SALTWATER COWBOY

LAURA RUDACILLE

INFINITY
PUBLISHING

Copyright © 2010 by Laura Rudacille

ISBN 0-7414-6187-0

Printed in the United States of America

This is a work of fiction. Names, characters, places, and incidents either are the product of the author's imagination or are used fictitiously. Any resemblance to actual events or locales or persons, living or dead, is entirely coincidental.

Published October 2010

INFINITY PUBLISHING
1094 New DeHaven Street, Suite 100
West Conshohocken, PA 19428-2713
Toll-free (877) BUY BOOK
Local Phone (610) 941-9999
Fax (610) 941-9959
Info@buybooksontheweb.com
www.buybooksontheweb.com

For Adam, Mason, and Teague

Acknowledgments

Kristen Kline thank you for your unwavering support, endless hours of journal gibberish translation, and my poolside va-va-voom head shot.

Tina Ruppert your strength as a single mom inspires me almost as much as your dedication to the environment.

Carin Kohlbus thanks for devoting your free time to endless hours of tedious editing and offering insightful suggestions.

Garrett Hartman, my cover collaborator and talented nephew, thank you for sketching until I had all the pieces I needed!

My impatient-for-the-final-copy preview readers, Mom, Carol, Christine, Diane, Pam, Tonya, and Kristen. The evolution of the manuscript couldn't happen without you.

Above all, thank you Adam, Mason, and Teague for loving lazy laid back vacations and being patient while I obsess with adjectives and artwork.

SALTWATER COWBOY

CHAPTER ONE

Murphy rarely left his Montana ranch for more than a few days. He never took vacation, and by no means, a trip that involved an airplane. But when his best friend Joel's appendix burst and he asked for a favor, Murphy could hardly turn him down. It turned out the favor involved two weeks on the eastern shore island of Chincoteague, rounding up wild ponies for a fund raising auction.

A holiday at the seashore wouldn't have been Murphy's first choice, but the truth was he needed a break. His sister, Tory, had said she'd sedate him herself and hog tie him to the plane if he didn't get away for a while. "The ranch will still be here when you get back Murphy," Tory said. "We can handle the horses. Besides, I'm tired of you sulking over that no good filly. She didn't break your heart; you haven't even had it stolen from you yet."

Maybe Tory was right…The filly in question wasn't the four legged variety, but a bombshell blonde he had met at the rodeo the year before. A six month firestorm of passion ended when she eloped with a champion bull breeder leaving Murphy crushed as effectively as if he'd been thrown carelessly from the back of a thousand pound bucking bronco.

Despite her tearful pleas for understanding, Murphy had carried his shattered ego back to the ranch and buried his misery in the back-breaking tasks he loved. He shook his head mirthlessly as he remembered. Blind and stupid was not a ride he planned to repeat.

So all in all, as it turned out, Joel's appendix couldn't have had better timing.

Within two days, Tory had booked Murphy's flight and packed his clothes; Joel had arranged the rental house and handled what he deemed necessities, and Murphy dutifully did what he was told.

He'd disembarked the plane and was met like a celebrity by a driver holding a card with his name neatly lettered in bold black print. It was approaching midnight when the hired driver delivered Murphy to the door of the rental house. Joel's provisions were detailed in a folder on the kitchen counter; a map of the island, a rental car, a daily itinerary, and a fully stocked refrigerator. Murphy plucked a cold beer from the top shelf and decided the rest of Joel's arrangements would be better appreciated in the morning. He found the couch, pulled off his boots, and gratefully put his day of travel behind him.

The following morning, with a solid five hours of sleep under his belt, Murphy crossed the shelled parking lot and faced the Atlantic Ocean. He'd purposely come at dawn figuring a 'full day at the beach' meant sunup to sundown. According to Joel's itinerary, Murphy had a few days until his round-up duties began so... vacation.

Murphy tossed the shade umbrella the clerk assured him he would need into the sand alongside a small cooler. He unfolded his beach chair and planted the legs in the soft beige sand. The aluminum frame was still wrapped in protective plastic, and the cardboard price tag tossed in the ocean breeze. He settled into his chair and flipped open the cooler lid... Water, check, reading material, check, and sunscreen, check. What else could a day at the beach require? He opened his magazine and prepared to relax and enjoy the day.

A few fishermen stood in the surf; their rods held high as the undertow swept their baited lines to the fish below. The sea rolled past them and rushed over the sand to where their tackle boxes and bait coolers sat safely onshore. Murphy shaded his eyes against the glitter of daybreak as it danced across the ocean's surface. "Looks easy enough," he muttered, "Might have to give it a try." Silhouetted against the horizon, two kayakers pulled themselves through the swells a few hundred yards from shore. "Cool... I wonder where I could rent one of those," Murphy said to himself.

Gradually the sun lifted to the sky. The fishermen disassembled their gear; the kayakers were mere dots on the horizon. The beach filled with people. Murphy watched with amazement the magnitude of *stuff* the vacationers dragged from their cars. These serious beach goers brought wagons overflowing with umbrellas, chairs, coolers of impressive sizes, totes of sand toys, EZ-ups for shade, snacks, boogie boards, skim boards, surf boards, body boards, floaties, sand mats, blankets, towels... "Unbelievable," Murphy murmured. The chaos was entertaining and surprisingly soothing, so Murphy decided to enjoy the show.

About 10:00 am Murphy slathered coconut scented sun block across his legs. His sister Tory's voice replayed in his head. "It's a different kind of sun in the East, Murphy. Buy sunscreen and **use** it." He chuckled as he remembered Tory smiling through her tears as she shoved him toward the gate at the airport. "Have fun," she had said as she hugged him firmly. "What could be better then herding wild ponies alongside the ocean? And just think of the scenery... blondes...bikinis..."

Tory had been right about one thing, the scenery was terrific. Right now he was watching a stunner in a polka-dot bikini. Her hair dangled in long, wet, red spirals down her back. Problem was that she was about two-years-old. Her mom and dad were working tag team to keep her from racing head-long into the ocean. The little girl carried her sand-pail to the sea, filled it with frothy water, and then giggled with every step as she returned to shore. Time after time the tot dumped the saltwater onto the beach, and then rushed into the surf yet again.

Murphy leaned forward to retrieve another bottle of water from his cooler. He had scooted his chair under the welcome shade of his umbrella. Okay, so the clerk had been right, he was grateful for the shade. He had sat and thumbed through his magazine; he'd dozed and taken a walk; and still it was barely mid-day. How people could repeat this day after day for an entire week dumbfounded him. The hours passed, early birds packed up, sun worshipers reapplied oil, and turned their chairs to follow the arcing sun. Murphy observed the sixty year old man in cut off Levi's reclining in a sand chair a few yards away. A beach lifer for sure, the sun bounced from his oil slicked body. The man's skin had taken on an orange-ish bronze color that reminded Murphy of well oiled leather. Murphy considered, as the man turned to his belly like a rotisserie chicken, "In a few more years, he'd make a fine saddle."

Murphy tossed his water bottle into the cooler. He had seen enough and decided to call it a day. He would head back to the rental house for a shower and then try the Bayside Inn for a seafood feast. As he levered himself from his chair, he saw her.

She moved gracefully through the bodies sprawled across the sand. Sandals dangled from her fingertips and a hemp knapsack hung simply over her shoulder. The ocean breeze ruffled her loose linen pants and pressed her untucked t-shirt tight against her body. The wind played with her shoulder length brown hair as she scanned the shoreline selecting her spot.

Murphy lowered himself back into his chair and decided a few more minutes of beach time wouldn't kill him.

The woman dropped her sandals, dug a towel from her bag, and sat cross-legged without a care on the smooth sand. She smiled openly as the children raced the receding waves, and then laughed as they squealed when they got caught to close to the next crashing crest. Intrigued, Murphy watched her cuff her pant legs and roll them until they hedged above her knees. She leaned back on her hands and tipped her face to the sun. Several minutes later,

4

she spread out her towel and pulled a novel from her tote. Lying on her side, her cheek resting on her palm, she flipped open the book and began to read. The wind fought with her pages, but she didn't seem to mind. Idly she drew circles in the sand with her toes, and when she tucked a stray piece of hair behind her ear, the sparkle of a simple gold earring winked in the sunlight.

Murphy wasn't sure he had ever seen anyone so at peace. No pretense, she was completely at ease. Sunglasses shielded her eyes and Murphy itched to know what color they'd be. He knew he was staring but he couldn't tear his gaze away. Her hair wasn't really brown; it was a concoction of color, tawny, russet, even streaks of gold. Not a product of a fancy salon, but sun kissed flawlessness. A healthy outdoor tan brushed over her muscled calves and arms. Murphy would have bet a grand that she worked outdoors. Her only visible frill was a flirty purple polish that tipped her toes. He watched as she stifled a yawn, and stretched her arm out across the warm sand. With her head cradled in the crook of her elbow, sleep claimed her.

Waves continued to lull and the sun crept toward the horizon. Beach goers trudged through the heated sand to their vehicles. The beach was nearly vacant and still she slept. Murphy picked up his chair and dragged closer to the sleeping woman. Guarding her, not stalking, he told himself; as he set up his chair and flipped open his magazine. Curious, he glanced over at her and felt something tip in his chest. How could a sleeping stranger pull at him without a word? Maybe his sister had been right. Maybe his heart hadn't been taken from him after all.

The sounds of the ending day trickled into her dream, urging her to surface. "Oh..." she groaned in weak protest as she rolled to her back. Her sunglasses slipped up to her forehead. Absently she removed them and stretched fully across the towel. "Hmm," she hummed and turned to her side. Murphy watched her stir and settle back in. He willed her eyes to open just to answer that one simple question. Like magic, her eyes flashed open. Clear and focused, she observed Murphy as he studied her. "Morning," She said with a lazy smile and hoped she didn't have drool rolling down her chin.

"Green," He said in a deep rumbling voice.

"Excuse me?"

"Your eyes. I've been wondering... brown, blue, hadn't considered green."

Nervously she replaced her glasses and although he was disappointed, he reached out a hand. "Hi, I'm Murphy Keen. I'm not a stalker, even though it may appear that way."

She shifted to her knees and stretched to reach his hand, "Jess...Jess Thomas." Much like he appeared, his hand was rough, strong, and all male. Tanned face, sandy blond hair, at first glance, you'd think surfer. A weathered t-shirt stretched across the lean rangy muscles in his shoulders and arms. But it was his untanned legs that gave him away. "Cowboy?" Jess asked as she stuffed her towel into her tote.

"I believe the correct term is Saltwater Cowboy," Murphy smiled. "But I'm a first timer, so I could be wrong."

Passing through, Jess thought with a twinge of regret. Better that way, she had no time for tangles with a man, regardless of his appeal. Jess stood quickly and gathered her things. "You'll have a busy week. Good luck," she said, as she started to stride from the beach.

"Where are you hurrying off to?"

"Got things to do," she called over her shoulder.

Murphy tossed his magazine and towel into his chair and folded it all together like a beach chair burrito. "Hold on Jess." His long legs ate up the distance as he hurried after her. "Want to go to dinner?"

"Not a stalker Mr. Keen?" Jess laughed.

"No, really. I was going to get some dinner and thought you may want to join me. Bayside Inn?"

Jess sized him up. It had been months since she allowed herself any leisure time as a female. What could it hurt? He'd be gone in days and he was certainly pleasing to look at. "You're on Mr. Keen, but I'll warn you, I am starved, so bring your wallet. I like to dance, so wear comfy boots, and I have integrity, so I will not be sleeping with you. No funny business."

"Sounds fair," Murphy smiled, enjoying her. "And Jess, it's just Murphy."

"Alright, just Murphy, I'll meet you at the Inn in an hour."

"See you there," Murphy said as she strode across the crushed shell parking lot to a white Jeep.

Jess tossed her tote in the back, grabbed the roll cage above the driver's side and hoisted herself behind the wheel. Murphy watched as she pulled a ball cap from the gear shift and stuck the bill between her teeth. Her fingers raked through her hair and with a quick flip and twist, Jess threaded an unsecured ponytail through the back of the cap. The Jeep roared to life, *Bon Jovi* pulsed from the stereo, and she rolled out of the lot.

Murphy rubbed his hand across the ache in his belly, recognizing the tug of lust. He had fallen flat before and blind and stupid was not something he planned to repeat. This time he would open his eyes and use his head. He was simply going to enjoy a meal, a dance, and no sex with her after all.

CHAPTER TWO

One hour later, Murphy strolled across the wooden dock which led to the open air restaurant and bar. The Bayside Inn was a landmark of the island. His buddy, Joel, had assured him that this was the place for food, booze, and music while he was in town. Not much for wandering aimlessly, Murphy was grateful Joel had pointed him in the right direction. He chose a stool on the end of the bar where he could see the pier as well as the dance floor. The barmaid moved over as he settled on the stool. Murphy ordered a beer and flipped the mousetrap that was secured to the oak bar in front of him. Unique.

The waitress set the frosted glass bottle down and turned up her most inviting smile. "That mousetrap," she explained, "is to hold your money tight to the bar against the bay breeze." She batted her lashes.

Happy there wasn't a rodent problem, Murphy took a swig of beer and studied his surroundings.

Jess had watched him stroll in as if he were a regular, exuding that male confidence that could easily have been mistaken for arrogance. Murphy had smiled at Zoe, the pretty young waitress, nodded to a scruffy, fresh-from-the-boat first-mate, and then with an easy manner, he had pulled out a stool and ordered a beer. Murphy's genuine nature was obvious. Jess smiled at his confusion when the mousetrap puzzled him. That threw most people the first time. He had just begun to scan the bar when his blue eyes zeroed in on her. The punch of his smile should require a license, Jess thought. She nodded carefully and Murphy was striding towards her before she had a chance to regulate her racing heart.

She had tossed on some jeans and a fresh white t-shirt, Murphy noticed. Her hair was tied back from her face but other than that, she was beach Jess. No fuss, no extra polish, just woman. "You were early," Murphy said as he slid a hip on the stool beside her.

"Shocked?"

"Is there a safe way to answer that and still be a good guy?"

"Are you a good guy Murphy?" Why was she flirting? Jess scolded herself as his grin flashed again. She was not skilled enough for this game. The last thing she wanted to do was to give Murphy the wrong impression. Jess decided a polite lie to excuse herself before the evening became far too complicated would be best.

"Do you know who Kate is?" Murphy asked, interrupting Jess's plan for retreat. "I called ahead for a table." He noted the flash of surprise in her eyes. "I wasn't sure if we needed a reservation and you did say you were hungry. I didn't want us to have to eat at the bar."

"Starved," Jess corrected as she angled her head toward a robust woman moving from the kitchen with a loaded tray of food. "That's Kate." Murphy gauged the woman to be late-fifties, although he was horrible at presuming such things. What did it matter anyway? Murphy had always thought you had one life and that was not nearly enough time to grow, learn, live and love.

"Hello Jess, Handsome," Kate winked at Murphy, "You call for a table?"

"Sure did," Murphy said easily.

"There, in the corner," Kate inclined her head. "Settle in, I'll be along in a jiffy." Kate smiled and without an ounce of discretion allowed her gaze to absorb every inch of Murphy's body.

Jess laughed as his cheeks flushed pink. "Watch out for that one."

"I almost feel violated," Murphy choked with humor.

"She's harmless, really." Jess laughed richly. "Come on, follow me." He did and hoped he'd figure out a way to make her laugh again. They settled at the plastic table along the framed glassless windows by the water. The salty bay air rushed from the water, sweeping through the bar.

"Those mouse traps are making sense now," Murphy said. A fishing boat eased up alongside to the dock. The captain issued orders from the control tower and the mates scampered to tie-off and secure the vessel to the pier. The chartered fisherman climbed to the dock and sidled up to the bar. The day's fishing stories circulated, and the simplicity of island life was enjoyed by all.

Jess and Murphy sat back; their conversation flowed easily. Kate took their food order and brought fresh bottles of beer. Jess talked of how she had come to the island three years before to work for the National Parks Service educating children. In addition to her teaching duties Jess maintained the habitat for the hundreds of migratory birds that stopped on the neighboring isle, Assateague, throughout the year. She told Murphy about the wildlife circle where tourists could walk or bike throughout the wetlands and view the different species of birds and animals. Murphy listened intently over their salads wondering if she was aware how much passion she held for her work. He took note and added the wildlife loop to his mental list of things to do in the next two weeks.

As their entrees arrived, Jess stopped talking and laughed nervously, "My gracious, I haven't stopped talking since we sat down. You must be bored to tears."

"Not at all, but I do understand why you passed out so soundly on the beach today." Murphy scooped a fork full of lump crab from his plate. "Mmm, this is incredible."

"The Inn's crab cakes are superb, but try this." Jess hooked a penne noodle, speared a scallop and a shrimp, and lifted her fork to his lips. Murphy closed his mouth over the fork. Jess's eyes tracked down realizing the intimacy in the simple gesture.

"Wow you're right," Murphy said hoping to put her back at ease. "Thanks for sharing."

A large boat pulled to the dock. Mermaid Encounter was scripted across the side. Mid-party, the rowdy crew secured the lines and set up chairs on the boat deck. The young bartender, Zoe, hustled over and leaned out the framed window with an order pad in her hand. Whistles and jeers followed as the boisterous crew was open with their flirtation. Zoe smiled but handled herself. She blew the crew a playful kiss and sauntered away to fill their order. Murphy laughed and raised his brow at Jess.

"Hard day at sea followed by good music and happy hour," Jess explained, and shook her head. "Zoe better watch herself with that crew."

Jess leaned back in her chair and rubbed her stomach. She had plowed through nearly every bite on her plate. "Ha," she laughed heartily, "I told you I was starved. Now you'll have to let me digest and then we'll dance these calories off." A buzz sounded and Jess's hand flew to her hip. She lifted her cell phone and looked at the display. "Sorry Murphy, I have to take this." She excused herself and ducked down a hallway for privacy.

Kate, the seasoned waitress, returned. "Well Handsome, what'd ya think?" She gathered the dishes efficiently.

"Best crab cake I've ever had," Murphy said.

"Next time go for the soft shell crab."

The thought of eating anything still inside its shell made Murphy queasy. It must have shown on his face. Kate hooted out a laugh, "That spun your guts!" Her laugh wheezed out. "You come again and try it. I'm wrong, it's on the house." Jess strolled back around the corner. "You bring this girl with you when you come. She doesn't make enough time for herself." Kate turned to Jess, "How's your man?"

"Great. He's busy getting the corral ready."

Murphy wasn't pleased at the swift stab of jealousy.

"Enjoy the music, you two," Kate said. "They should be starting any time now."

"Katie!" The rowdy boat's captain called out. "Are you on the menu tonight sweetheart?"

"You could never afford me," Kate cockily shot back causing the crew and listening bar folk to laugh. Jess leaned in and spoke quietly to Kate. Murphy watched as the women exchanged one of those female looks before Kate wandered off.

Jess settled at the table. "Everything okay?" Murphy asked her.

"Yeah, The Captain has a thing for Kate. He's harmless but when he's had a few..." Jess's eyes shifted to the boat tied nearby. "It's fine... I'm just over protective."

Murphy laid his hand over hers. "Sounds like you're a good friend to me." Jess glanced down at his strong hand. It was a simple thing really; the comfort and understanding that his gesture offered. Jess's eyes moved from their joined hands to Murphy's face. Nothing simple or basic there. He was stunningly gorgeous. His strength radiated in an intoxicating drag-you-off-to-the-cave kind of way. Jess's fantasy life had always been rich but as Murphy's grin slid into place, she shut down the Bam Bam reverie and pulled her hand away.

The band started behind them. Murphy rose, "I'll get us another round. What would you like?"

Jess looked at her watch, "Another beer, then water, please?"

"You've got it."

The music was great. A local group, Jess told him. A long haired drummer about fifty-five, a twenty something surfer on lead guitar and he'd guess a thirty year old tanned beauty on bass. They had an extra mike stand in the center and every few songs, someone from the crowd would walk up and join in the vocals.

"Pretty cool how everyone knows the routine." Murphy leaned in close so Jess could hear. She had turned to face the band. Her feet were propped on a vacant chair, and her toes tapped in time. She was as vibrant an energy as Murphy had ever seen.

The guitarist waved her to the microphone. Jess grinned but refused. "Not tonight," she mouthed to him.

"You sing?" Murphy asked.

"Usually, but not tonight," she tucked her heel under her tush and gave Murphy her full attention. "Tell me about you. How did you get to be a real cowboy?"

Murphy looked into Jess's green eyes and found himself compelled to give the long version of his story. "I grew up in a small town in Pennsylvania. Typical childhood, I guess; soccer, school, and best friends. My sister Tory and I would fly out to my grandparents' farm in Montana each summer for two weeks." He leaned forward on his elbows, "How could you not love that?"

Jess smiled at Murphy, pleased when he continued on.

"My parents' divorce came out of nowhere. Mom decided to move all of us to her childhood home so we could have a fresh start. My grandparents were the rock my mother needed when divorce turned our world upside down. They gave Tory and me everything, but most of all, they provided us an opportunity to build fulfilling lives." He was quiet for a moment. "It's a ready made family on the ranch." Murphy grinned at Jess. "I got uncles, aunts, and cousins overnight. None of them blood, mind you, but when you sweat alongside a man or share a hard earned breakfast, you build bonds that far exceed birthright."

"Family's vital," Jess nodded.

"Yes," Murphy agreed. "The ranch healed us. Our summertime crush quickly grew to true love. Mom remarried a few years ago, and she and her new husband travel the world." He chuckled, "I usually don't know where she is." Jess laughed with him. "Tory and I were in our twenties when we realized the ranch was what we wanted for the long haul. We decided to dig in and commit."

"Big undertaking at twenty," Jess said.

"At twenty, you're fearless, right? World is yours to do anything with."

Jess sat quietly thinking over her own decisions at that age. "Yep, I know what you mean. So how are your grandparents handling ideas from the younger generation? It had to be an interesting transition for all of you."

"Grandpa was all for it. He helped me pick a few horses to start a *Keen* line. Tory worked with Grandma and expanded the stable to include boarding, kid camps and riding lessons. Their greatest passion was rescuing neglected farm animals and rehabilitating them. My big sister has a soft spot for the mistreated so we added a pasture for her rescues."

"Sounds amazing," Jess said with admiration. "Do your Grandparents still play an active role?"

Sadness came into Murphy's eyes, "They died about a year ago. Grandma went first in May, and then six weeks later, Grandpa."

Jess reached out and stroked his arm. "That's so sad, Murphy. I'm sorry."

"Always harder for the ones left behind, yeah. Hours before my Grandpa passed, he gave me the greatest gift. He told me he had spent a lifetime of living and loving fully. He told me that he and Grandma, how did he put it?" He considered a moment, "He said that Grandma went on ahead and their hearts required each other in life and in death." Murphy sat quietly, "I wish everyone could have known them."

Jess's heart tipped at the loyalty and depth of his feelings for his family. "How are you here Murphy, in my puddle of the world? How did you come to be a Saltwater Cowboy this season?"

"Joel, my best childhood friend, helped out with the round-up on a dare in college about six years ago and has helped out every year since. He said there was nothing like herding wilds in the sand. Every year he begged me to come and I never committed. The ranch has demands that can be unpredictable." He shrugged.

"Wait a minute. I think I know who you mean." Jess's brow creased as she searched her memory. "Joel, the mechanical contractor from Pennsylvania?"

"That's the one," Murphy smiled. "Anyway, Joel's appendix blew last week and he asked me to come. He didn't want to leave the firefighters a man down. I am going to check in at the firehouse tomorrow and talk with Chief Rudy. I assume there are a lot of things that need doing before the actual week of the auction."

"You'd be right." The music shifted to a *Bon Jovi* song and Jess surged to her feet. "Calorie burn time Murphy." She wiggled her way through the dancers. Murphy took a deep breath and followed her in.

A few songs later the tempo slowed and Jess looked at Murphy, "Want to get some air?"

He simply took her hand and pulled her toward him. "You didn't say no slow dances, Jess. Let's just enjoy one and then take a walk."

She sighed as he reeled her in. This was all too easy. The cynical side of her was clawing to the surface. Murphy felt her tense. He lowered his head to her ear and said, "Relax sweetheart, I heard you loud and clear earlier today, it's just a dance."

A little unnerved at how well he was reading her, Jess tipped her head up at him and smiled shyly, "It's just been a while Murphy." They enjoyed the music and got a bonus when the first song simply rolled into another. The song ended and the tempo kicked up and Jess stepped back. "I need to get going."

"Let me clear the tab and I'll walk you out." In the parking lot they stood beside her Jeep. The sky was clear and full of winking stars. Jess caught Murphy looking up and smiled. "Missing home?"

"Just the opposite actually. I'm thinking I need to call my sister and thank her for insisting I make the trip." He smiled and stuffed his hands into the pockets of his jeans. It had been an effortless evening. He couldn't remember ever having such an easy time with someone. He was sorry it was ending. "I hope we can see each other again while I'm here."

Jess tossed her tote into the back of the Jeep. "It's a small island. I think we'll bump into one another." Why was this always her luck? A terrific guy drifting through. Just once, she wished the cards would fall in her favor. She kept her voice light. "Thanks Murphy, I had a great time." Her eyes locked on his.

"I had a great time too." He leaned in intending to buzz her cheek, but on impulse, decided he could keep it simple and still go for the lips. Simple, simple he repeated in his head. The brief contact did nothing but foster his interest in her. He eased back. Not simple, definitely not simple. Jess stood before him, eyes closed, holding the moment. When her lids blinked open, her green eyes were blurred.

Instinctively she leaned toward him. Her hand raised but instead of gently touching him she pressed her palm to his chest. "Whoa there Jessie," she said on a whisper. Murphy watched her rein in. Jess's gaze traveled from where her hand rested over his heart until she absorbed every inch of his face. His chiseled features gave nothing away as he studied her in return.

He was right out of a Stetson advertisement, tall, rangy, and undeniably sexy. Jess had convinced herself this part of her life was unnecessary. A hormonal indulgence was not worth the price of the life she had worked so hard to build. Her hand vibrated over his thundering heart. The resolve she had taken years to build fell away like chunks of a glacier. In a split second her fingers fisted the soft cotton of his t-shirt, and she launched herself at him.

She pounced like a mountain lion. Murphy barely pulled his hands from his pockets fast enough to keep them both upright. However this night ended, it certainly wouldn't be in a tangle of limbs on a crushed shell parking lot. Her assault was relentless, not that Murphy was complaining. Jess's hands moved to his shoulders, then his hair as he angled his head allowing her to take more. Murphy gripped her hips and tightly fused them together. He was drowning on dry land and prayed no one would save him.

As suddenly as she had leapt, Jess jerked free and shakily stepped back. "Murphy ..." Her finger tips traced over her lips. "It has been a perfect evening and it's been a long time since I ..." Would he stop gaping at her like she was a lust starved woman who had attacked him shamelessly in a parking lot? Jess straightened her spine rigidly. "I won't apologize."

Murphy saw her lips moving but the blood had left his brain.

"Forget it." Mortified, Jess whirled around to get in the Jeep.

"What? Wait... Jess?" Murphy shook his head clear in time to realize she was bolting. He stepped forward and caught her hips. "Jess?"

"No," her voice quivered. "No. I need to go. Now."

"Jess," he repeated softly.

"Please Murphy, I need to get home."

"In a minute," He turned her around but she wouldn't look at him. "Hey, I heard you. I know what *No* means, alright?" Murphy tipped her chin until her eyes met his. He was determined to end their evening on a positive note. "Jess, I had a great time and I hope I will run into you again."

She gazed at him. He was, *this was,* a mistake. She worked out what she needed to say. Finish this before it started. "Murphy..."

"That sign says karaoke is tomorrow night. Will you be singing?"

He was letting her off the hook. A gentleman too... great. What kind of resolve would a woman who has seen no action in seven years have against a man like Murphy?

"Jess?"

"Yes," she sighed "I will be singing tomorrow." She shook her head, "Murphy..."

"You said you wouldn't apologize, Jess. Please don't. I had a great time and I will look forward to hearing you sing tomorrow night." Murphy leaned in and kissed her forehead lightly. When he would have stepped back, Jess stopped him by hooking her fingers in the belt loops at his waist.

"I'm not a gambler Murphy. I have too much to lose."

"You had conditions for this outing. How 'bout we set up some for tomorrow?"

He had surprised her again. "Okay Mr. Murphy," she snickered. "Let me think. Here we go... I will be here tomorrow night because I was planning on it. I'll sing because I like to, and I have integrity, despite the wild animal attack you just endured, so I won't be sleeping with you." A quick cocky grin followed and Jess rose up on her toes and planted a swift kiss to his lips. Laughing she jumped behind the wheel and Murphy watched her pull out of the lot just as he had earlier that day.

Man, she was some puzzle, and damn if that didn't intrigue him more. Not blind or stupid this time, yet an ache deep inside mocked him, as her Jeep's tail lights disappeared from sight.

CHAPTER THREE

Murphy padded barefooted to the kitchen. The rental house was over the top, just as Joel had promised. Casual décor, luxury feel. The home was located at the end of a dead end road. Stilted off the sand as most coastal homes were in defenses against storms, the quaint two story had a wrap around deck and huge windows overlooking back bay. He could see the water that separated Chincoteague Island from Assateague Island through the window over the kitchen sink. According to Joel, the ponies would be swimming across the channel just a few miles from the house.

Murphy opened the fridge and pulled out eggs, orange juice and fresh ground coffee. He had more than enough food, thanks to Joel. Not a bad deal, other than he'd have to cook it himself.

Joel had also given Murphy some websites to check out to fill him in on the island's history before getting on the airplane. In the early 1900's the young community of Chincoteague relied on the mainland fire company for safekeeping. Following a devastating blaze in 1925 which destroyed a large portion of the town on Chincoteague, the island residents decided to start their own fire company. In 1946 the federal wildlife refuge system granted a permit to the fire company allowing them to keep 150 adult ponies on the Virginia portion of Assateague Island. Maintaining the size of the herd was necessary and profitable. The proceeds benefited the volunteer fire company and would be applied to the purchase of new fire equipment. The pony penning evolved over time to include the swim, and was enjoyed by staggering crowds annually.

The house phone rang, piercing the peace of his morning. Murphy took a guess, "Morning Sis."

"Hey, you psychic now?" Tory chuckled. "How is it going, how's the house? Is the beach pretty?"

"I'd love to pull your leg and tell you it's awful but actually it's great." Murphy thoughts drifted to his evening with Jess, "Really great."

"Are you eating?"

"As we speak," he flipped his eggs over and tuned off the heat. "Joel had the fridge stocked and an itinerary on the counter when I got here. I'd be surprised if he didn't arrange for maid service too during my stay."

"He's so glad that you went. I talked to him last evening. He is so bummed that he is not there with you. He asked me to tell you to call him after you meet Buzz. Who's Buzz?"

"My horse, I think." Tory laughed and updated Murphy on all he missed at the ranch in the last twenty-four hours. "I'll be fine," Murphy said when she finally wound down. "Actually you were right and don't gloat. I needed a break Tory, I needed this. Thanks for pushing me on the plane. Now my eggs are done and the only thing I love more than you is food. I'll talk to you later."

Murphy carried his plate to the deck and enjoyed his breakfast as the morning sun danced across the bay. There were birds along the water's edge combing the soft sand for some breakfast morsels of their own. Farther out fishing boats bobbed on the choppy surface. "Therapy," he muttered and forked up some eggs, "for no extra charge."

Just shy of 9:00 AM, Murphy strolled into the firehouse. His boot heels clomped and echoed down the long tiled hall. He followed the sound of voices to the recreation room where several men of varying ages were shooting pool while ESPN played on the flat screen. A college stud spotted Murphy first. He propped his cue on the floor and molded his body in that casual *screw off* posture kids mastered by the age of twenty. With his graphic t-shirt stretched tightly across his over-trained pectorals, 'College stud' nudged the bald man next to him and said, "Rudy, here's the cowboy."

Rudy was the fire chief of Station forty-four. He was nearing retirement age and from what Murphy could see, Chief Rudy was incredibly fit.

With an impressive wad of tobacco rammed in his cheek, Chief Rudy turned and smirked as his eyes tracked over Murphy from his ancient cowboy hat all the way down to his well worn leather boots. He lifted a tin can from the edge of the pool table, pressed the can to his lips, and spat. Chief Rudy sat the make-shift spittoon down and rubbed the back of his hand across his mouth.

Murphy held the Chief's impassive gaze as they sized each other up. Tension hummed throughout the room. Chief Rudy cleared his throat and handed his pool cue to 'Studly' who squirmed inwardly, but mentally took detailed notes on the masculine display.

"Joel told me to expect a soft, aged, pudgy, wannabe cowboy sometime this morning," Rudy jeered. "You him?"

The men stared a moment longer, Murphy shrugged, "That'd be me." Simultaneously, their faces split into broad grins, and as it was with most males, ribbing, belching, and practical jokes were a rite of passage. Camaraderie was instantaneous. Handshakes and introductions followed and Murphy was accepted into the clan.

Chief Rudy gave Murphy a tour of the station. The front room had been transformed into a gallery of Pony Penning photographs. Years of snapshots and professional photos were displayed artfully across the walls.

Murphy was drawn to one image which captured a Saltwater Cowboy clinging to his mount as it boldly reared in the surf. The back drop for the pair was an endless summer sky dressed in the unbelievable hues of the setting sun. Murphy leaned in and read the brass plate fixed below the picture, *Rudy and Scout, 1983 Pony Penning.*

"Great photo. You've been at it awhile."

Rudy grinned, "More years than I will admit most days."

"Your horse is a beaut," Murphy noted.

"Scout was one of those once in a lifetime horses. I believe he and I were soul mates of a sort."

The men stood in silence and paid homage to Scout. Murphy knew the bond between horse and rider was sacred. Chief Rudy led Murphy from the room. Murphy glanced over his shoulder at the array of photos and added a return trip to the gallery to his list of things to do before he left the island.

At the end of the hall Rudy stopped by an open door. Music pumped throughout the well lit room. Murphy glanced over an array of fitness equipment, nautilus, elliptical trainers, and free-weights. Rudy took a single step into the room, drawing the full attention of the men utilizing the apparatus. "Our Cowboy," he announced. They raised their hands in welcome. Chief Rudy gestured to the room, "Help yourself if you feel the need."

Murphy nodded, "May just do that, Chief."

"Plain ol' Rudy suits me, if it's all the same to you. Let's get you over to the fairgrounds." The men drove to the fairgrounds a few blocks away. Rudy explained that the ponies would end their journey in the corrals located there on Wednesday morning. After separating the weaned foals from their mothers, the auction would begin early Thursday morning.

Rudy eased his truck into the fairground parking lot. "So," Rudy said as they climbed from the truck, "I'm taking you backwards, which is my nature." He reached into his hip pocket and pulled out a pouch of leaf tobacco. Wadding a large ball, he stuffed it into his cheek, then offered the pouch to Murphy who declined.

"Never took," he said with a shrug.

"Better for it," Rudy led Murphy into a small stable. "Buzz is one of my best." A whinny followed and a buckskin head poked over a stall door. "Heard me big guy?" Rudy allowed the horse to nuzzle his bald head. "Softening me up aren't ya' boy? He loves me." Rudy grinned at Murphy, and discreetly slipped a palmed sugar cube to Buzz, "Almost as much as he loves my sugar."

Tethered to the rail of the corral, Buzz stood alert as Murphy ran the soft brush over his neck. He talked constantly to the horse as he moved competently around Buzz.

Across the corral Rudy groomed a black quarter horse, Onyx. He stroked the shiny pitch colored coat and watched Murphy closely. You could learn a lot about a man when he worked around animals. This man, Rudy surmised, was composed, uncomplaining, adept, and kind. And that, Rudy decided, worked for him. He hoisted a western saddle from the rail and walked toward Murphy. "Let's load 'em up and hit the sand."

Rudy drove across the bridge between Chincoteague and Assateague, parked in a large lot, and saddled the horses. He pulled a can of bug spray out and enveloped himself in a cloud of toxic mist. "You'll need a little of this," Rudy tossed Murphy the can. Murphy made a face and Rudy laughed. "Trust me on this one; it's no slam to your manhood, Son. 'Round here the mosquitoes got big teeth." Murphy sprayed his pants, his arms, then removed his hat, as he had seen Rudy do, and doused that as well.

The men led the horses to a shaded trail and mounted. "We'll take the wildlife loop and let you and Buzz get a feel for each other," Rudy said.

A sign at the entrance posted no motorized vehicles until 4:00 pm. One lane of macadam, wide enough for a vehicle, wound through the grassland, marsh, and forest. Murphy was certain this was the nature loop Jess had spoken of over dinner. It was early in the day, and the heat of the rising sun hadn't reached the oppressive temperature of the season. People rode bikes, jogged, or strolled leisurely enjoying the morning. A young child tested his training wheels while his father ran with open arms behind him. The clatter of the spinning crutches along the pavement would surely frighten any wildlife away long before a sighting was possible.

Thirty minutes into their ride, Rudy veered Onyx off the path onto a soft sandy trail. The men and horses wound through deadfalls of trees. Squirrels, rabbits and an occasional muskrat peeked at the horses and riders invading their sandy home. Murphy stopped counting the different species of birds perched in the trees or skimming insects from the boggy pools of water. A rustling drew Murphy's eye in time to see a chestnut dappled rump scampering from the underbrush.

"You ever see one of those?" Rudy asked.

"Sika?"

Rudy nodded approvingly as the small bodied relative of an elk disappeared into a thicket.

"Only on the Outdoor network. They're small." Murphy shielded his eyes in an attempt to locate the buck in the brush. "Lost him, great camouflage."

"Quick and skittish, makes 'em a kick to hunt. Over on the northern side of Assateague you can get license and hunt the beach. Got some whitetails up there too."

One more thing to look into, Murphy thought. His list was growing. Rudy stopped Onyx and Murphy pulled Buzz alongside him. From the top of the dune they had a full view of the open beach. The men sat in silence and absorbed the unblemished scene. "Beautiful, ain't it?" Rudy said.

The northern edge of the island was only accessible on foot, bike, or horseback, so the beach was unoccupied. It was nothing like the barrage of people Murphy had waded through the day before. "Every part of the world has magic. This is spectacular."

Pleased with his reaction Rudy smiled. "Hey Murphy," he taunted, "Catch me." Rudy flicked the reins and Onyx shot off across the sand.

Murphy gave Buzz a nudge, "YA!" Without hesitation the horse galloped after Onyx. Rudy raced along the surf where retreating waves splashed beneath Onyx's pounding hooves. Murphy leaned over Buzz's neck, urging more speed from the horse. After a mile the riders eased up and the horses fell to a trot and then a relaxing walk.

The ocean orchestra surrounded them. The waves crashed and raced ashore tossing glistening shells carelessly in the salty mist. Gulls overhead screeched in annoyance at nothing in particular as they floated on the constant wind off the water. Sand pipers on short legs chased the receding frothy water, plucking unseen specks from the sand. Nature's perfection; Murphy soaked it all in.

Rudy's tanned face was split with a boyish grin, "Can't get this out west."

"Nope, you sure can't," Murphy agreed.

Jess had been working all morning roping off a section of beach where the *Plovers* were beginning to nest in the sand. As she attached a sign warning visitors that this remote section of the beach was closed, she noticed the riders in the surf. Rudy, she recognized immediately, and even at this distance, she knew it was Murphy beside him. He sat tall in the saddle, his long legs fixed strong in the stirrups. Still some distance away, Jess took a minute to control her hormones. "It was dinner and a kiss, well two whopper kisses, but come on Jess, chill out." By the time she'd fixed the final caution sign, the men had made the turn out of the surf and were headed in her direction. Jess leaned her shovel against the Nature Center ATV and pulled bottled water from the cooler she had strapped on the rear bumper.

"Jessie darlin'," Rudy shouted and lifted his hand in hello.

"Hey there Rudy, you breakin' in the new guy?" Jess called.

"How'd you know he's new? He's got a solid seat." Rudy might have been old but he wasn't slow. The look that zipped between Murphy and Jess was blistering.

"Afternoon Jess," Murphy touched the brim of his hat.

"Murphy," Jess said with a shy smile as she walked to Buzz and rubbed his nose. Buzz nipped the top of her water bottle making Jess laugh that full bodied laugh that Murphy had yet to chase out of his head. "You need a drink big guy?" She murmured to the horse.

"Wouldn't turn one down," Rudy teased.

"I've got bottled water on ice in the cooler," Jess said, as Rudy dismounted and dropped Onyx's reins on the hot sand. "There are two gallons of spring water behind the seat if you want to water the horses."

"Cool toy," Murphy eyed Jess's ATV.

"It's a work vehicle," she said primly.

"Jessie, Jessie," Rudy shook his head. "It's oversized tires strapped to an engine. Flying sand...speed."

Jess snorted, "You men are all the same, boys in grown up bodies."

"Damn straight." Rudy hefted a gallon jug of water and moved off to water Onyx.

Murphy eased from the saddle and tucked the reins into his back pocket. "What you working on way out here?" He asked Jess.

Jess explained about the nesting grounds, and pointed out an area where the *plover* nests were barely visible in the soft sand. Murphy listened intently as she explained the process applied to help keep the vulnerable eggs safe. Murphy felt a growing admiration for the individuals who dedicated their careers to protecting something most people would trample over without ever seeing.

"When you guys moving the herd?" Jess asked Murphy.

"Starting tomorrow, right Rudy?"

"Yep, tomorrow," Rudy stowed the water jugs in the ATV. "Singing tonight Jess?" Rudy asked.

"I don't see any reason not to."

"Your man coming along?"

"Can't carry a tune without him," Jess teased. Rudy caught a glimpse of Murphy's jaw tightening. Some things were hard for a man to hear. Better to find out sooner than later, Rudy had always thought. Not his place to get involved. He lifted Onyx's reins. "Thanks for the hospitality Jess. We need to get on. I want to show Murphy what wild ponies look like in a marsh."

"Bug spray?" Jess raised her brows.

"We're men." Rudy swung into the saddle, "Bug spray's for sissies." Murphy threw his leg over Buzz and settled into the saddle.

"Suit yourselves. I'll see you later, if there's any meat left on your bones." She watched the men move north over the dune. Murphy's Levis hugged the saddle in a way that had Jess humming. Rudy was right; Murphy did have a great seat.

As the horses moved toward the island's interior Murphy noticed other areas that were protected by ropes. He read a sign warning vacationers of nesting sights as well as informative plaques depicting the types of birds visible in the area.

Rudy gave a low whistle drawing Murphy's attention. Up ahead in the tall marsh grass, a small herd of fifteen ponies stood encompassed in the sea of lush vegetation. A gust of wind moved the tall reeds of beach grass in undulating waves. The vibrant greens were broken by older dried shafts of tan and an occasional burst of pink and white from a large bloomed wildflower. The ponies' tangled sun-bleached manes hung long over their strong necks. Their tails and ears twitched in constant motion to deter biting flies and mosquitoes.

Murphy's eyes were pulled to a painted mare with a nursing foal. Their splattered white and brown markings were nearly identical. What a picture the cluster of ponies made as they grazed in the open marshland.

"Pretty sight, huh Murphy?" Rudy beamed.

"Sure is."

"Enjoy your last hours of peace, boys and girls," Rudy pulled out his tobacco pouch. "Tomorrow, we're coming to get 'ya."

The men finished their ride and returned the horses to the fairground stable. Murphy decided to take Rudy up on the offer to utilize the firehouse fitness room and ran to his rental house to change clothes. He figured it would be a good way to meet more of the firefighters he'd be riding with over the next few days.

Murphy hopped on an elliptical trainer and punched the preset warm-up program. As expected, several men were exercising throughout the gym. Their conversations bounced between them, and Murphy knew he'd pick up a lot, just listening.

Bobby, about twenty-six, was getting married in a few months and had an opportunity to make an offer on a waterfront property. He gripped a pair of forty pound dumbbells and worked his triceps while he asked an older man he called Nub about mortgage rates. Across the room, Sean, the college stud, was a fourth generation Volunteer Fire Fighter on Chincoteague. He'd been helping with the Pony Penning festivities since he was six years old and had even purchased a pony himself. He and another firefighter, Rocco, were currently spotting Gus at the bench press. Murphy noted the weight mounted on the bar and realized the grunts weren't all for show. After completing the final rep, Gus sat up and caught the towel Sean threw to him.

"Damn Gus, you put us to shame, dude," Sean scoffed.

"Not all of us," Rocco faced the mirror and struck an impressive pose.

"You want guns Sean?" Gus stood sandwiching Sean between him and Rocco. Gus pinched Sean's arm then growled as he flexed his enormous biceps. "You got to put in the time Puny."

Sean glanced in the mirror at his arms and frowned. He'd been secretly squeezing in additional workout sessions, and thought he'd seen an improvement. Next to Rocco and Gus, he looked like a gangly pubescent.

"Besides," Gus winked at Murphy, including him in the mischievous banter, "I heard Zoe likes the muscled type. Maybe I'll ask her to the steamer tomorrow night."

Rocco joined the roast, bumping Gus aside so he could flex his chest and arms posing like a professional bodybuilder. "Me and Gus could give her an invitation to the gun show." The men displayed their sizable arms taunting Sean.

Murphy swallowed a chuckle as he watched Sean attempt to remain composed. His fists were clenched tightly at his sides as the muscled duo continued to bait him mercilessly. Sean lost his battle for self control and lunged for Gus.

"Easy, Puny," Gus spun Sean effortlessly and pinned his arm behind his back.

Rocco danced like a prize fighter and jabbed Sean softly in the ribs. "Don't make us make you say 'uncle' in front of our Cowboy." Face red from embarrassment as much as fury, Sean wriggled and strained to escape Gus's iron clad grip.

"You gonna' behave?" Gus asked. Sean relaxed and nodded his head. "Really Sean," Gus released him and lifted a water bottle from the bench, "I didn't think you were serious about Zoe."

"Seriously twisted up," Bobby piped up from across the room. "He hasn't made any moves on her, the way I hear it."

Sean's gaze zipped from one person to the next as they gave him grief. Zoe had worked at the Bayside Inn since she was sixteen. Niece to the owner, Zoe had started working as a hostess, moved to waitress, and now that she'd turned twenty-one, took shifts behind the bar. Sean had been watching Zoe for the better part of six years. When he was near her, he felt like an idiot school boy. His tongue would triple in size. He'd stutter, or worse, just stare at her and say nothing at all. Sean felt like a bigger fool because everyone knew he was interested in Zoe, except Zoe. Recently when he'd stopped at the Inn after his shift, Sean had witnessed the men at the bar noticing her. More disturbing than that, Zoe hadn't seemed to mind their attention.

Frankly, it ticked Sean off.

Murphy pitied Sean as the ribbing from his fellow firefighters rained down.

"You want to be her man Sean, you better throw your hat in, that's all I'm saying," Gus said. "Now, hit the shower, Puny. Tonight just might be your night."

When Murphy heard Gus say "her man" he felt a jealous fire flicker inside him. Kate had asked Jess about *her man* at dinner, and Rudy mentioned it again on the beach. Jess had answered them casually enough but she also had kissed the brain out of his head just as easily. He had no business even dwelling on it, yet it festered just the same. Maybe it was all the talk about hot women. Murphy punched the intensity up a few levels on the elliptical and decided a hard workout would be the ticket to settle his mind.

Murphy had finished cardio and was hitting the free weights when Rudy wandered into the fitness room about an hour later. Rudy recognized male frustration when it was sweating right in front of him. He ambled toward Murphy and decided to get to the root of it. "We had ourselves a nice ride today didn't we Cowboy?"

"Sure," Murphy snapped curtly.

"My men treating you alright?"

"Yep."

"Must be a female then."

"Uh-huh," Murphy huffed and dropped the weights into the rack, and picked up his towel. "What?"

"Too late," Rudy chuckled. "A man working out as hard as you've been is aggravated 'bout something. You're on a vacation, of sort. Just came back from an exceptional ride on God's most beautiful island. My men are too smart to piss off an extra pair of hard working hands. So my logic tells me, your problem is female." Rudy glimpsed Murphy's scowl a moment before he whipped his towel from his shoulder.

"God's most beautiful island huh?" Murphy wiped the sweat off his face, "How many islands you been on?"

Rudy studied Murphy seriously before he muttered, "One."

Sean and Bobby walked back in to the gym on the heels of Rudy and Murphy's laughter. "What'd we miss?"

"None of your business girls," Rudy tongue lashed the men.

Sean cleared his throat, "Hey Murphy, you coming to the steamer tomorrow night?"

"I'm not sure what a steamer is, but I've got no plans."

"Steamer is tradition after the first day of herding. It's the best damn meal on the planet," Rudy said.

"I'm in," Murphy said.

"We could be feeding you dung and fish gills for all you know," Rudy quipped.

"I won't have to cook it," Murphy said and the men laughed again.

CHAPTER FOUR

The cool air-conditioned house washed across Murphy's heated skin. He almost preferred the sweltering humidity that saturated the island to the artificial arctic. "Beer then shower," he muttered as he pulled open the fridge. "And maybe some music too so I quit talking to myself." The note Joel had left said 'hit play and the stereo will take care of the rest'. Sure enough the elaborate sound system obliged Murphy's mood by kicking out *Jimmy Buffet*.

Cold beer in his hand, bare feet braced wide, Murphy stood framed in the huge glass patio doors. The late afternoon sun tipped toward the horizon urging the lazy shadows of shoreline trees to creep across the bay.

The water was quiet but for a lone fisherman piloting a small aluminum boat. Murphy watched as the man systematically cruised to his marker buoys and hauled wire crab traps from the water. The solitary fisherman worked unhurriedly as he emptied his catch into baskets onboard the boat. He worked the bay water until his line of buoys led him to disappear from Murphy's view around the edge of the cove.

When *Buffet* rolled over into classic *Kiss,* Murphy grinned. Joel had preprogrammed all of his favorites. "Took care of everything, didn't you? Stinks that you're laid up buddy." Murphy muttered and tipped his beer only to find it empty. "Drinking alone, talking to myself..." He shook his head, walked to the kitchen, and set the bottle in the sink. The light on the phone was blinking. Murphy crossed over, punched the button, and Tory's voice floated out:

Hey there little brother, just checking in. Your cell phone flipped me right to voice mail so I thought I'd try you here. Everything's fine on the other side of the country. Joel says, according to the normal schedule, you'll be herding tomorrow. Don't forget your sun block. Love you... Try to check in with Joel, he's feeling down, not being there with you.

Murphy picked up his cell phone, bemused that he had tossed it on the counter the night before and spent the entire day without it. "Must have needed a vacation more than I realized." He keyed in Joel's number and after a few rings Joel picked up.

"Hey Murphy, how's it going?"

"Not too bad," Murphy answered. "How ya healing? Everyone's asking about you. The guys were hoping you'd feel up to coming over for the final cookout."

"Right now I'd have to say not a chance. My sorry butt is dragging."

"I'll let 'em know."

"How do you like the house?"

"Awesome doesn't cover it and I am baffled as to how you arranged the preprogrammed stereo, but there is one problem."

"What?"

"You really overshot the groceries. Exactly how many people were you planning to feed?"

"Herding makes you hungry, but actually I hoped you'd find some beach babes and have yourself a co-ed barbeque. You did see that hot tub on the deck didn't you?" Joel snickered.

Joel's laughter was music to Murphy's ears. "Wild plans bro."

"Don't disappoint me, I am going crazy in this bed," Joel said. "I am sick of feeling sick. Give me details bud; I need to live vicariously."

Murphy and Joel spoke for nearly thirty minutes. As he hung up the phone, Murphy decided to skip the shower and take advantage of the hot tub.

Pruney and relaxed, Murphy pulled on a pair of soft lounge pants, grabbed the television remote, and stretched out across the king sized bed. He had only a few moments to appreciate the big screen mounted over the fireplace and vast space the room offered before his eyelids drooped and he was fast asleep.

Energized from his cat nap, Murphy pulled his rental car into the jam-packed parking lot at the Inn. "Take their Karaoke seriously." Murphy squeezed the sedan into the last available space, and then strolled across the lot and onto the wooden deck planks which led to the bar. A siren's voice called across the night air beckoning all men within earshot to their imminent doom. The bar was wall to wall bodies. Rather than attempt to find a vacant stool, Murphy decided to lean against a pillar on the outer rim of the mass. Cutting through the lively crowd wearing a face encompassing grin was Kate.

"Hey there Handsome, I hear you had a nice ride and got to see our island."

"News travels," Murphy smiled at her.

"Small island. Beer?"

Murphy nodded and Kate moved briskly toward the bar. The song ended and applause rang out. Next, a group of men and women took their turn. Little talent, but they obviously felt safety in numbers. Thankfully the karaoke jockey only had three microphones so the not completely tone deaf dominated the noise.

The crowd clapped enthusiastically as Kate made her way back to Murphy. "Here you go, Handsome." Kate stepped beside him and leaned heavily on the wooden column. "I'm due for a break. Tell me about your ride."

Murphy filled Kate in on the beauty of seeing the wild ponies in the marsh, and the exhilaration of racing the horses through the surf. As he spoke, a female voice, soft and pure, began to sing Carrie Underwood's latest hit. The formerly rowdy crowd hushed, and focused on the singer who could have easily been professional. Intrigued, Murphy found himself straining in vain to see the stage.

"She's quite a package, our Jess." Kate said quietly.

Murphy stared at Kate, unsure he had heard her correctly. "What?"

"Jess," Kate inclined her head toward the lighted area. "Voice of an angel."

Murphy pushed from the pillar and muscled his way to get a clear view. Jess stood with her hip propped on a stool. One hand on the microphone, her eyes closed, she moved through the song's second verse. The crowd swayed along as the stirring notes of the chorus ripped from her throat. When Jess finished, bar goers surged to their feet and appreciative whistles and cheers roared through the night air. Murphy stared at Jess. A ghost of a smile peeked at her unpainted mouth, yet her gaze never rose from the floor.

"Duet, duet, duet," The gang chanted.

Murphy's stomach clenched as Jess's face changed dramatically. Her expression radiated genuine affection, as her eyes tracked to someone in the crowd. The rowdy bar patrons cheered as Jess stretched her hand into the audience and said *"come here, my love."*

The DJ cued the song and *Summer Lovin'* boomed from the speakers. Murphy stretched to see the man, *her man*, but failed to edge the dancing bodies out of his way. His vision was monopolized by Jess's face as she sang adoringly to her partner.

Kate had moved to Murphy's side. She watched curiously as he tried with great effort to see Jess's duet partner. It would be interesting, Kate mused, to see his reaction.

The song neared the end. Jess bent down out of sight. When she and her man hit the final note, the crowd separated and Murphy saw her hugging a small boy against her side. Murphy squinted and shook his head to clear the image. Whatever he had expected, a child hadn't been it.

"Surprised?" Kate asked Murphy.

"I'm not sure what I am." Murphy answered honestly.

"They make a picture, don't they?"

Kate's comment rebounded off Murphy's broad shoulders as he moved to the back of the room toward the pier. She angled her chin and frowned at his retreat. "Certainly hadn't pegged you for a coward, Handsome."

On the pier Murphy stood and looked across the water. "A child," he muttered, "twisted my guts inside out, over a child. Boy, I'm stupid."

"Talking to yourself Murphy?" Jess swaggered toward him, "People will get ideas about you." He stared at her through guarded eyes. She accepted the analysis. Men could be so fickle, especially to a woman who was also a mother. She had heard all the excuses from polite to ridiculous. Which would Murphy offer, she wondered.

"Your voices are nearly identical, did you know? Probably won't be for long with puberty..." Murphy trailed off. What was he saying? Was he even making sense?

Jess's mouth dropped open in shock.

"Momma?" Feet pounded the deck planks. Jess spun around and kneeled just in time to catch a bundle of energy as he launched himself into her arms. "Can I go with Rudy to check the pens? Please Momma, please."

"Hush now," Jess stayed level with the boy and turned to look at Murphy. "Riley, I'd like to introduce you to a real cowboy." The boy's green eyes lit with interest. "This is Murphy. He has a ranch in Montana. Murphy, I'd like you to meet my son, Riley."

Murphy studied the small freckled face with eyes that matched his mother's. "It's a pleasure to meet you, Riley. I enjoyed your song."

"I wanted to sing *Def Leopard* but Momma likes the sappy stuff."

Jess rolled her eyes and eased to her feet. "Riley, where are your manners?"

"In my other coat."

Jess snared Riley in a playful headlock, "You little smart mouth."

Murphy's laughter rumbled out at their horseplay.

"Just kidding, Momma," Riley said quickly and held out his hand to Murphy. "Nice to meet you, Mr. Murphy."

Murphy gripped his tiny hand, "Just Murphy."

"So Momma can I go?" Riley bounced on his toes.

"I need to talk to Rudy first."

"He said to tell you to skip the dance for once." Riley mimicked Rudy's tone and inflection like a seasoned impressionist. "He said," Riley continued, "Tell your momma I got it covered and stop frettin'. Sing a little and boogie with the cowboy." Riley eyed Murphy, "That'd be you, I take it. Do you dance?"

Murphy swallowed his chuckle, "On occasion."

"Well young sir," Jess scrubbed Riley's curly hair. "Frettin' is my job." She grasped Riley's hand, squared her shoulders, and faced Murphy. "You hanging?"

Murphy understood the underlying question masked within. "I'm not going anywhere, Jess."

Her shoulders relaxed and that easy smile Murphy liked so much slid across her face. She nudged Riley with her hip and said, "Take me to your leader." Riley snickered and raced down the planks.

Murphy's beer dangled forgotten at the tips of his fingers. He tipped his head up to the star lit sky and breathed deeply. He was rarely caught off guard and couldn't decide if he was intrigued or irritated. The cool bay breeze washed over him, settling him. Bit by bit Murphy became aware of the music, lights and bustling from the barroom a few yards away. His boots moved seemingly on their own propelling him across the scarred strips of weathered wood.

Kate looked over as he walked back into the noisy room. She was busing the table he had shared with Jess the night before. "Grab this one while you can." She pointed to his empty bottle, "Another?"

"Please...but I don't know what Jess is having."

"Water, most likely, with Riley underfoot."

"Scrap the beer then Kate, and bring me water too."

Kate squeezed his shoulder, "You're a good one, aren't you Handsome?"

"Depends on the day," Murphy tossed her a wink and slid into the chair.

"Ha!" Kate barked and moved toward the bar wishing she was twenty years younger.

While Murphy waited for Jess, a woman painstakingly murdered a *Stevie Nicks* classic. The buzz of the bar picked up and mercifully muffled the singer's unseemly pitch. Kate bustled over with two glasses and a full pitcher of water with lemons floating among the ice cubes. "Whew, Meg can kill a great song better than anyone I know."

Murphy chuckled.

"Here comes our dove."

Jess slid into the chair across from Murphy. "Sorry that took longer than I expected," she said. "Thanks Kate."

"My pleasure, where's your man?"

"Rudy stole him for a few hours."

"Good, now you two enjoy the music." Meg hit an ear shattering high note and Kate shuddered. "Well...enjoy the rest of the music." She disappeared into the crowd.

Jess eyed Murphy, "You need the full history or just the facts?" She reached for her water and sipped slowly as she studied him over the rim.

She was used to getting the third degree about Riley, he realized. "Neither, what did you do today?" Murphy watched the surprise on Jess's face soften and erase her prepared defense. Visibly relaxed she folded her arms on the table's edge, tapped her fingers in time to the music around them, and told him about her day.

From behind the bar, Kate watched the two of them. She had never considered herself a voyeur, but she couldn't help herself. Her heart lightened as Murphy reached over to refill Jess's water glass. It floated higher still as Jess leaned across the table as if sharing a secret. When a patron hailed Kate from the end of the bar, she nearly cursed. Perhaps she was a bit of a voyeur after all.

More singers took their turn at the microphone. The karaoke DJ called out Jess's name. The crowd cheered in anticipation. "You mind?" Jess asked Murphy.

"That was one of the conditions right? You'd sing because you like to."

"Brace yourself," Jess said as she stood and took a sip of water. "This one is a request."

It's Rainin' Men blasted from the sound system. The women in the bar sang along, and pumped their fists in the air. When the song ended, the chant 'duet' rang out again.

Jess raised her shoulders regretfully, "I've lost my partner," she apologized and hopped off the small stage. Murphy watched as she wound her way back to their table. It was obvious she loved singing but was a little uncomfortable with the praise.

The evening passed much like the night before. Boats came and went, people stayed and moved on. Jess looked at the display on her phone noting the time. "I need to get going Murphy."

"Yeah, me too," Murphy followed her through the bar. He noticed curious looks and murmurs that spurred in their wake.

"You're giving me a reputation." Jess giggled, as they crossed the shelled lot. "I can hear them chatting now, *Two nights in a row that girl's left with the Cowboy.*" She laughed again, "Just one of the splendors of a small community."

Despite her laughter, Murphy wasn't entirely convinced. "I don't want to cause you any trouble, Jess."

She leaned against her Jeep and smiled knowingly up at him. "You may be the kind of trouble I need." Without hesitation Jess grabbed his shirt and hauled him against her.

She braced herself for that exhilarating punch of power, and it came. But as Murphy's arms surrounded her, an easy sigh escaped her lips and she softened as the kiss slipped blissfully away.

"Jess," Murphy nipped her lower lip. "Jess," he whispered again and rested his forehead against hers.

"I know... but I won't apologize."

"Damn your integrity," Murphy chuckled tightly. "Now I don't want to spoil the moment, but I do have one question about Riley."

Jess tensed immediately. Here it comes she thought, just when she'd dropped her shield. A glint of steel laced her eyes as she raised her chin and focused on Murphy's face.

Murphy's chest constricted as he accepted her scrutiny. What did she think he was going to ask? "Is Riley's father in the picture?"

"His father?" Jess blinked and shook her head. "No unfortunately or fortunately depending how you feel about it. No, he is definitely not in the picture."

"Just wanted to know how many players were on the field."

"This particular game has been called for foul weather for several years."

It pleased him to hear it, yet it made him sad thinking how difficult it must have been for Jess to raise her child on her own.

"Murphy, Riley is my man. He has been my man for the last seven years and I can't, won't," she affirmed, "do anything to compromise that."

Murphy took her hands and held them. His heart tripped in his chest as she stared warily up at him. *She's waiting for me to bolt, like a skittish horse,* he realized. "Do you get any mornings off? I'd love to take a ride on the dunes with you. Maybe Rudy could lone us a mount."

Jess studied him carefully. She was never sure what to expect from him. Her phone buzzed at her hip. She tipped the screen so Murphy could read it. 'MY MAN' flashed in the ID box. Jess flipped open the phone and "Hey Riley...yes I'm on my way...That's not necessary...Alright if he's sure it's no trouble. See you in the morning, I love you angel." Jess smiled at Murphy. "Rudy is letting him sleep at the station. He's become like a grandfather to him since we moved here. You want to go back in?" Jess motioned to the bar.

"And have to exit again?"

"That would feed the rumor mill wouldn't it?"

"I would like to spend a little more time together if that's okay with you." It may have been several years but Jess recognized the intense heat in Murphy's eyes.

"NO," Jess stepped back abruptly and thudded soundly against the side of the Jeep.

"Careful," Murphy snickered at her. "I told you I know what that word means and I happen to remember rule number three. Let's just take a drive."

Jess started to refuse but knew she'd enjoy showing him the island especially at night. "Where are you staying?"

"Deep Creek Landing."

"I'll follow you. We'll drop your car."

She started their tour with the island's northern most point. More remote, the northern tip had undeveloped acreage available for sale. The bay front properties boasted quaint store fronts and mom and pop retail shops handed down from generation to generation. Novelty souvenirs, hand dipped ice cream, salt water taffy, and fresh squeezed lemonade; the quaintness of the small community was unmistakable. An hour later, she pulled the Jeep through the gate of Nonan's Marina where boats of all sizes bobbled alongside floating wooden docks. "This is as far South as Chincoteague goes." From the lot they had a clear view where snippets of big business were in the early stages of development. Profitable shoreline properties were appealing and a handful of chain hotels were in the early stages of construction. "Three years ago I'd have sworn that you'd never see a big chain hotel on this island."

"The lure of big money creates monsters."

"You got that right." Jess eased the Jeep on the main road. They drove past the US Coast Guard Station. Murphy marveled at the size of the cutter docked along the pier. Jess made a few turns and soon they were traveling slowly down a tree lined road. Murphy had lost track of which direction they were headed. "Riley and I rent back here. Rudy owns the cottage. I think his family has owned this land for years. Anyway it suits us." Jess angled the Jeep into the drive. The sweep of her lights showed a white Cape Cod with a screened in porch. "I need to let my pup out. My lawn is treated for mosquitoes but you still might get munched." Jess raced to the porch. Murphy climbed from the Jeep and looked over the property. Tall trees sheltered the cottage from the road. A narrow shell covered path wrapped around the side of the house. Lit by solar lights the pathway led to a dock where a small aluminum boat was tethered.

"Heads up," Jess called a second before a rocket of fuzz shot from the screened porch. "PONCHO!" Jess raced behind the dog who was on a collision course with Murphy.

Murphy turned quickly. "**Sit.**" He commanded firmly. Poncho skidded to a stop and plunked his furry bottom on the ground.

"Good dog," Murphy said and the dog head tipped his head to the side. "Boy? Girl?"

"Boy," Jess said, "with no manners." Poncho looked at her from where he sat obediently at Murphy's boot, "Usually."

Poncho's entire body quivered with excitement. Murphy leaned down and rubbed the pup's head. Without an ounce of pride Poncho flopped to his back as if to say *gimme more buddy*. "You are a good boy aren't you?" Murphy stood. Poncho hopped up and raced off to take care of his business. "This is a great spot Jess. You do any fishing?" Murphy nodded toward the boat.

"Sometimes I take Riley and go out, but not often. You plan to do any bay fishing while you're here?"

"I've been compiling a list. So far I've got surf fishing, kayaking, wildlife center, pony photo gallery, looking into permits for Sika hunting, and now, bay fishing."

"Add in your round up duties and the festival and I think you will have an exhausting two weeks."

"Down to eleven days already."

"Maybe you'll just have to pace yourself and come back another time."

"What do you do with Riley while you're working?" Murphy asked.

"He spends his days with a friend of mine. She's a teacher at the school so she has her summers off. She has two boys a few years older than Riley. He gets his male bonding with a mother with *testosterone experience* supervising." They both laughed. "The boys all hope to be Saltwater Cowboys someday. This year Rudy's allowing them to pay their dues. The boys will be preparing the stables and corrals, hauling straw and hay and my personal favorite, scooping poop during the parade."

"Good for them," Murphy said. "There's nothing like working hard to earn what you want." Poncho raced to Murphy's feet and dropped a gnarly stick on top of his boot.

"Poncho, we aren't staying to play." Jess picked up the stick. The dog shifted his attention to Jess and barked excitedly.

Murphy grinned down at the persistent fur-ball. "Go on Jess, toss it for him."

Jess hefted the stick through the air, then smirked at Murphy, "You have no idea what you've started. This dog doesn't quit. We'll be out here for hours."

"We've got time Jess," and Murphy promised himself he'd make the most of it.

CHAPTER FIVE

Murphy sat on the rise of dune on the northern part of Assateague. He counted roughly thirteen foals and twenty adult ponies in the lush reeds that covered the marsh. He had ridden all morning with the volunteer firefighters he had met the day before. Murphy hung back and watched Nub, Gus, Bobby and Sean move deftly through the tall grass and surround the herd.

The ponies scatted in confusion as the riders invaded the marsh. Murphy spurred Buzz and circled the flank to pick up any strays. After the disruption the ponies grouped together in comfort, and slowly, the wranglers encouraged them from the marshland.

Gentle, yet firm, the part-time cowboys gave Murphy the impression they moved livestock on a daily basis. The men urged the ponies to the beach and into a large temporary corral. Veterinarians evaluated and aged the foals, while organizers drafted a list of youngsters available for auction. Murphy admired their system which seemed perfected to the smallest detail.

Once the ponies had been catalogued, the Saltwater Cowboys herded the group to their permanent holding corral located along the main access road. It was a long, slow walk up the beach, but Murphy had no complaints. The foals hugged their mothers' sides and followed dutifully along.

Sean eased his mount beside Murphy and Buzz. "What do you think, Murphy?" He said companionably. "Are we living up to Joel's recommendation?"

"He's never steered me wrong," Murphy smiled. "Have to say I'm looking forward to the swim."

"Yep, that's pretty great." The horses plodded along the shoreline. "Up ahead we need to tighten ranks a bit. The people will be lined up, excited to get a snapshot, as we bring them in. Ponies usually don't mind much, but you always have one or two sightseers that push for an exclusive." Sean scoffed.

"Got it, thanks Sean."

A moment later, Rudy called out for the men to cinch together just as Sean had said. The Saltwater Cowboys ushered the ponies through the maze of camera wielding folks and hurried them into a lush grove. The gates swung wide and without causality the ponies moved hastily inside.

Fresh straw scattered across the shaded enclosure soothed the exhausted ponies. The high wooden fence provided a safe environment ensuring locals and tourists an ideal interactive experience with the wilds. Prior to the swimming event later in the week, teams of cowboys would continue to comb the island until the entire herd had been accounted for and secured.

Rudy and Murphy leaned comfortably over the top rail of the enclosure. Mares nursed their foals settling them in after the upheaval of the day.

"Ain't much prettier than a brand new foal," Rudy said.

Murphy nodded in agreement. The painted colt whose markings dittoed his mothers stood with his nose in the air. The young foal eyed Murphy boldly.

"Someone's got your number," Rudy chuckled and spat a stream of tobacco juice into the grass.

"He looks young to be weaned," Murphy said.

"He'll be a fall pick up I figure." Murphy looked curiously at Rudy. "Foals that aren't weaned still get sold. We keep them and their mothers on the fairgrounds until October. Owners pick up the foals in the fall, and then we return the mares to the herd for winter," he explained.

"Incredible arrangement you've worked out." Murphy complimented.

"Years of mistakes make us look smart," Rudy grinned. "Looks like we've got about half of them, not bad for the first day," Rudy stepped away from the rail. "Let's get Onyx and Buzz back to the stables. You bring a change of clothes?"

"Yep."

"We'll have us a steamer and celebrate the first day herding. You work up an appetite for dung and fish gills?"

·The color leeched from Murphy's face, and Rudy roared with laughter.

CHAPTER SIX

Murphy used the bunkhouse facilities to scrub off the layers of the day. His senses were bombarded by an intoxicating aroma as he stepped from the shower. He pulled on fresh jeans and a chamois shirt then followed his nose to the kitchen.

Several firefighters were working in teams, as they had on the dunes. Standing at a deep stainless sink, Nub and Rocco brushed the silks from fresh sweet corn; beside them two more men scrubbed red potatoes; and on a spacious granite countertop, Gus and Andy seasoned chicken breasts.

"That fire ready yet?" Rudy called from the center of it all. He had a chef's hat perched on top of his head, an apron tied securely around his middle with B-O-S-S embroidered across his chest. The men mumbled from their stations in response to Rudy's inquiry about the fire. "Murphy," Rudy zeroed in on Murphy's inactive body, "Stick your head out back and see if those 'knuckle noodles' have that fire ready yet."

"Knuckle noodles?" Murphy asked confused.

"Sean and Bobby," Rudy clarified, then jerked his thumb toward the door. We need that fire ready ten minutes ago." Rudy dismissed Murphy and turned his attention to the teams in the kitchen.

Murphy walked outside in search of the 'knuckle noodles'. The events in the backyard were a little less organized. Murphy spotted Bobby and Sean working on the fire pit in the far corner of the lot. Murphy chuckled as he approached Sean. Someone had taped a sign on his back which read, *I like men with big hoses.*

Murphy shook his head appreciating the practical joke. The air was intoxicatingly thick with lighter fluid fumes. "Hey Sean, Rudy needs a time on the fire."

"Would he just give me a minute, jeez?" Sean nearly bit Murphy's head off. "Ten minutes, tell him ten…" Flames leapt into the air and Sean ducked. "Shit Bobby, no more lighter fluid."

Murphy reported back to the kitchen, "Rudy, the boys need some more time."

"Nub!" Rudy hailed the senior firefighter and jerked his thumb toward the door, "Knuckle noodles."

"On it Chief," Nub bustled away to handle the boys.

Rudy barked another order and men hurried through the back door with tubs of scrubbed red potatoes. "Murphy," Rudy called, "Follow the guys 'round back. Tell the kettle men to layer the pricks heavy with seasoning, and get 'em in here pronto."

Murphy found Rocco with another group of men in the shade of the building with six huge cast iron kettles at their feet. Murphy relayed Rudy's instructions and with a nod from Rocco, the men hustled into action. Everyone seemed to know what the 'pricks' were and judging by the barrels of seasoning in their possession, layering heavy wouldn't be a problem. Curious, Murphy watched as potatoes were dumped into the kettles then dusted with the seasoning. Nub threw open the lid of an enormous white cooler revealing iced live crabs. Four men pulled on heavy gloves and shifted the dormant crabs to the bellies of the kettles. Nub supervised the dividing of the crabs and then tackled the task of shoveling on the seasoning himself.

"Rock salt, Old Bay, and a closely guarded blend of Rudy's herbs," Nub commented and heaped another scoop of spice into the kettle. The heat of the day stirred the semi-dormant crabs, "Quickly men or you'll get nipped."

Murphy switched his attention to the awakening crabs. The men grasped the crab's shell from the back avoiding their vicious claws, as they worked to layer the snapping bodies over the dozens of red potatoes. Inventive curses flew as the occasional blue crab got a grip on soft flesh. Murphy chuckled; he couldn't fault the crabs for trying.

When the men were finished, they split into teams of three, and threaded thick bamboo rods through the handle on each kettle. It appeared to Murphy's eyes like a well scripted tribal ceremony of some sort. The men silently hoisted the weighty metal to their shoulders, and processed slowly to the back door where the kettle's girth scarcely cleared the doorframe. Engrossed in the process, Murphy trailed behind, taking care to stay out of the way as he followed the men into the kitchen.

Once inside, the food prep crew tossed chicken, corn, and clams on top of the crabs. Between each food layer, amazingly, more seasoning was applied. Rudy oversaw the process as each kettle was burdened with fresh foods. Following a final inspection, the steamer pots were ready.

Rudy clapped his hands three times and bellowed, "Fire!"

The men in the kitchen responded with a single clap and a quick shout of, "Hup! Hup!"

Murphy grinned, realizing his thoughts of a ritual were not far from the mark. He eased from the kitchen to discover the backyard was beginning to fill with people of all ages. Laughter and gaiety hummed in the air in anticipation of the feast. Across the grass lot behind the firehouse, a large white tent had been erected. Beneath it, long tables sat end to end. Each table had been wrapped in newspaper and held wicker baskets of paper towels and wooden mallets every few feet. Another canopy housed the beverages for the evening; iced kegs, a soda fountain, and several coolers which were marked "water".

Murphy ambled across the grass lot to the corner of the property to check the 'knuckle noodles' progress. Sean and Bobby were struggling to muscle a large grate in place over the fire pit. Murphy had to swallow his snicker, as the breeze fluttered the pranksters' note unmercifully still attached to Sean's back. Nub stood with his hands on his hips supervising the boys. Sean grunted, Bobby cursed, but eventually the hapless pair high-fived when their task was completed.

"Well done boys," Nub clasped Sean's shoulder. "Well done."

Murphy watched Nub's hand as it slid slowly along Sean's spine until it rested on his butt... and squeezed. "I've got a big hose," Nub said suggestively and walked away.

"Hey!" Sean voice squeaked in notable falsetto as he leapt aside. "What's the deal man?" He spun around, affronted at Nub's behavior, "You catch that Bobby? What gives?"

Bobby solemnly stepped over to Sean and ripped the note off his back. With obvious effort he refrained from laughing as he handed Sean the scrap. Red faced and furious, Sean crumbled the paper and tossed it into the fire.

Within the hour the backyard was packed with fire fighters, their families and anyone directly involved with the penning. Murphy figured just about the entire island was in attendance. Rudy led the parade of kettles across the yard to the fire pit. The firefighters used the bamboo rods to lever the weight of the giant pots as they lifted them into position. Once the final kettle was settled, Rudy clapped his burly hands three times and shouted, "Steam!" The men repeated their earlier response, "Hup! Hup!" The yard quickly adopted a festive atmosphere and the party was officially started.

Nub dragged Murphy into a round of horse shoes. He hadn't thrown in a few months, but as a team, he and Nub held their own. After defeating Bobby and Sean, they were challenged by Gus and

Andy. Nub threw a ringer and he and Murphy became the team to beat. Rudy had been watching from across the lawn. He filled his beer and strolled toward Rocco, "Let's knock those two hot shots off."

The battle raged. Two wins each, the clash went to a tie break. "Give it up Cowboy," Rudy taunted. "This is my pit."

Murphy's shoe arced perfectly, despite Rudy's attempts to distract him, and the metal horseshoe landed with a loud clang and knocked Rudy's point earning shoe from the peg.

"Bastard," Rudy seethed. "Rocco you gonna' take this?"

"No Chief," Rocco concentrated and released the shoe. It flipped end over end until it slammed against the peg, swirled around the pole, and settled in the soft sand.

"Whoop!" Rudy hollered as the ringer sealed the victory. "Got you Cowboy." The men shook hands and Murphy was relieved to have a break.

In the kitchen Jess had her nose practically pressed to the window. She's watched the horseshoe duel for more than an hour while she helped prepare the salads and desserts. It was great to see the men harassing Murphy. She hadn't expected it to be any other way. He was one of them.

"Shoot," Jess said when Rocco's shoe spun around the stake.

"How's the action out there?" Kate peered out the window.

"Rudy and Rocco closed the deal." Jess said.

"Too bad, Nub and Handsome had a nice streak going." Kate soaped a rag and started to wipe down the counter. "Rudy will be checking the pots soon, and then we'll take the salads out." Kate carried dirty utensils and empty pie and cake pans to the sink.

"I've got this Kate," Jess flipped the water on and added detergent. "Go out with Rudy and make sure he doesn't overcook those crabs."

"Like he'd listen to me," Kate snorted as she dried her hands on her apron. "Damn fool of a man thinks he knows everything about everything most of the time," she muttered under her breath as she left.

Jess loved the way Kate and Rudy circled around each other. Rudy was a happy bachelor, and Kate, a vivacious widow. They were perfect for each other, but neither bothered to take the time to notice.

Murphy walked through the back door and found Jess elbow deep in sudsy water. "Kate said you needed a hand in here."

Jess looked over her shoulder at him, *yum*, her body hummed...but leaving in a week. She clamped down her primal reaction. "Kate is meddling."

Murphy laughed, "So she thinks we need a push does she?"

"She means well," Jess shook her head, "sorry, Murphy."

"Don't be, I'm not. I thought we were doing fine all by ourselves." He noticed a tinge of the sadness cloud her eyes. "Jess, is everything all right?"

Doing fine going where? She wanted to say, but instead smiled politely. "Everything's great. Are you ready for a fantastic meal?"

Murphy knew she had shut him down. He picked up a dishcloth and started to dry the pie plates.

"Murphy this is not how you want to spend your evening. Go out with the guys."

"You're right. I don't want to do dishes all night, but I figure if I lend a hand, we'll get done faster. Then I can talk you into helping me check off an item on my list." Jess raised her brow in that sassy way Murphy enjoyed. "The Pony Penning photo gallery, would you like to walk through and look with me?"

Jess thought of the people who'd been in and out of this station hundreds of times and never made the time to really look at the photographs. She found it incredible that Murphy was taking the time to enjoy something most local folks took for granted. "I would really like that Murphy."

As they dried and stacked the final cake pan, Riley burst into the room. "Momma, Rudy said I get to add the ice to the coolers and run the soda fountain if I scrub the grunge off my hands, arms, and face."

"Does he expect you to take a shower?"

"Can I?" Riley jumped up at down at the thought.

"No. Come here." Jess grasped the hem of his t-shirt and in a swift move had it up and over his head. She turned the sink on and dunked Riley's head under the spray. He protested half heartedly, clearly thrilled with the idea of having his bath in the kitchen sink. "Close your eyes," Jess said as she clutched a bar of soap and lathered him up face, neck, and arms. Murphy grinned as she handled the ball of energy.

"This is like when we wash Poncho," Riley sputtered.

"Yep," Jess shoved him under the water and rinsed. Riley squealed at the shock when she flipped the water temperature to cold.

"Cold Momma, cold!"

"Poncho doesn't mind the cold."

Riley shrieked again as the icy water slithered across his back. Jess pulled a fresh dishtowel from the drawer and wiped his small body dry. "Now listen to me Riley..." Jess waited until he turned his face to hers. "My backpack is in the Jeep. There is a clean shirt inside. Lay this dirty one on the front seat, put the clean shirt on, then find Rudy, and follow his directions."

"Got it," Riley started to leave the room stopped and turned, "Thanks Momma."

"No sweat," Jess folded the dish towel and noticed Murphy leaning on the counter looking intently at her. Jess shrugged her shoulders, "This is my life."

"He's a great kid, isn't he?" There was sincerity in his voice that pulled at Jess's heart more than his flattering words.

"What he is, is a handful..." Jess trailed off as Murphy slid around the counter toward her. The gleam of mischief tainted his gaze, "Murphy," her voice warned.

"Jess," He mocked her tone. "Why don't you rattle off the rules for tonight so we can look at the gallery before the food's ready?"

"Smarty," Jess snapped the wet towel at his belly. "The rules for tonight will be...I will look at the pictures because I want to, we'll enjoy a steamer and great company because we'd be foolish not to, and of course..." Jess wagged her finger at him, "I have my integrity, so no funny business."

Murphy grabbed her hand and led her down the hall to the gallery, "Damned integrity," he muttered. Jess tossed her head back and laughed heartily.

CHAPTER SEVEN

Murphy held Jess's hand loosely in his as they strolled along the gallery walls. They commented quietly, but for the most part allowed the pictures to speak for themselves. Professional and candid shots, which had been donated over the last eighty years, ranged from black and white images to vivid color. The frames varied from museum quality matted with photo glass to handmade from recycled barn siding.

"I think this is one of my favorites," Murphy said, when they came upon the shot of young Rudy atop a rearing Scout.

"He is something, isn't he?" Murphy leaned in and studied the photograph. "Sure would have liked to see him with that horse.

It was easy to see that Murphy had grown to respect Rudy, more than that; he'd fallen under the spell of the Pony Penning like so many others before him. "This event fits you Murphy," Jess smiled at him. "You know you're kinda lucky Joel's appendix burst."

Murphy looked down at her, "Yeah, I thought maybe he'd owe me, but the longer I am here, I think Joel did me a huge favor." Murphy took both her hands and turned her body toward his. "I was in a rut back home Jess... a serious sulking match." Jess raised her brow. "Another story," Murphy dismissed her unasked questions. "The fact is, I would have never made time to come here this year. Even when Joel called with the appendix, I dragged my feet. If Tory hadn't insisted, and my sister can insist like no one you've ever met, I'd never have climbed on that plane." Murphy's thumb traced lazy circles over the back of Jess's hand. He was quiet for a long moment, as if captivated by the sight of their linked fingers. Murphy closed his eyes, overwhelmed by how settled he felt in a room of photos with a woman he'd known for only a few days. "Jess…" he began and was interrupted by footsteps pounding down the hall.

"Momma!" Riley shouted. "There you are…whew." He skidded to a halt by the door out of breath and wiped his brow. "Rudy said to get your sassy tuckous to the table and bring the Cowboy with ya."

Murphy stifled a chuckle, as Riley raced away. The boy was a piece of work. Jess looked at Murphy and rolled her eyes. "You ready for a fine feast?"

"Lead the way."

Murphy had never seen anything like it. If he invited one hundred relatives over for a holiday dinner, this was probably what it would look like. A big noisy family meal. Jess sat to Murphy's right with Riley and the rest of the gang settled in around them. Murphy watched as the kettles were carefully drained and then turned over into huge aluminum bins. The fireman carried the bins, mounded with steamed food to the tables and the banquet began.

Murphy studied the newspaper draped table before him, unsure where he should start.

"Dig in boy, you wait, you starve." Rudy reached over Murphy's shoulder and dug out a handful of clams, an ear of corn, a chicken breast, two potatoes and of course a few crabs. "Gotta' stake your claim," Rudy snagged a wooden mallet from a bucket of utensils on the table, tore a few paper towels from the roll, and shoved them at Murphy. "Eat."

Murphy observed the folks around him doing just that. Sean munched on a golden ear of sweet corn slathered in melted butter. Boots ripped a little-neck clam from its shell, tossed it into the air and nimbly caught it between his teeth. Across the table, Nub held a steamed crab in front of his face and said, "Thanks for sacrificing your life, dude. I'll honor you by eating every bit of your tasty little self." Nub flipped a tab on the crab's hard shell and ripped it free with a practiced skill.

"Brutal," Murphy muttered as mallets smashed down with resounding thuds around him. Maybe he'd start with something easier, like chicken.

Taking his cue from those around him, Murphy pulled the chicken breast apart with his fingers. Plumped and moist from the heat of the kettle, the white meat had become infused with the flavors of all the foods in the pot creating a taste unlike anything Murphy had ever experienced.

Jess smiled over at him. She remembered her first steamer vividly. She had been a shy newcomer with a five-year old on her hip. She leaned toward him, "Figuring it out?"

"Mmm hmm, it's wonderful. I wasn't sure what to expect when they tossed all that stuff in together." He groaned as his teeth sank in again, "It's beyond delicious."

"Try a clam." Jess pulled a bowl of melted butter in front of Murphy. She plucked a clam from the pile and dipped it in the pool of butter and popped it into her mouth.

Following her lead, Murphy repeated the process. The bite sized clam had a salty sweet taste enhanced further by the magic seafood seasoning.

Murphy wiped a drip of butter as it trailed down his chin, "Messy, but good."

Riley leaned across his mother's lap, "Hey Murphy, you picked a crab yet?"

Murphy selected a crab and studied it. Whatever human had looked at this shelled creature and thought *dinner* must have been starved. The crab's blue shell had been transformed to bright orange after bathing in the heat and steam of the pot. "I don't know where to start," Murphy grinned at Riley, "but I am going to give it a try."

"I'll walk you through it," Riley said confidently. "Grab your knife, and stick it in the belly where the flap thing is." His little hands held a crab out demonstrating for Murphy.

Jess reclined casually in her chair and watched her little man lead the cowboy through the procedure. It was a slow and exceedingly muddled process, but Murphy listened intently as Riley instructed him. Jess felt her heart slowly somersault, her throat clogged suddenly with emotion, as she watched the two of them. "I'm going to get us more drinks." She said in a rush, and pushed her chair away from the table.

Kate had seen Riley's interaction with Murphy. More, she had seen the color leech from Jess's face a moment before she'd hurried from the yard. Kate waited a moment, and followed her young friend into the station house.

Jess leaned heavily over the kitchen sink; her head cradled in her hands. "Dumb, dumb, dumb," she repeated.

"Watch it; you're talking about someone I care an awful lot about."

Jess turned and moved into Kate's open arms. "Oh Kate, what am I doing?"

Kate gathered her in and held tight. "Being a woman, I'd imagine."

"Did you see how Riley looked at him? I need to go... I need to go home now."

"You are not a quitter Jess," Kate said gently. "Riley is getting along with Murphy just as he did with all the guys when you came here. This is no different."

"But it **is**." Her voice pitched in anguish. "It's different and complicated... I'm getting twisted up in something that has no potential. I will not give Riley false hope."

Kate stepped back and took Jess by the hand, "Come here." She tugged Jess toward the window, "Look there."

Murphy leaned away from the table with his arm draped across the back of Jess's vacated chair. Comfortable and completely at ease, he was laughing. A moment later, she saw why. Nub and Sean were taking turns tossing clams across the table for Riley to snag from mid-air. The men cheered as the boy caught three in a row.

"Oh, he'll be so sick." Jess said.

Kate chuckled, "He'll sleep like a rock." Maternally, Kate laid her hands lightly over Jess's shoulders. The women stood in the quiet kitchen, watching the scene through the glass. Kate turned Jess to look directly into her friend's worried eyes. "Just because a woman becomes a mother, doesn't mean she stops being a woman." Kate soothingly rubbed her hands over Jess's arms. "There are no guarantees in this life. Not one. I lost love much too early, but I loved."

Jess allowed Kate to tuck her under the comfort of her arm. Standing hip to hip they looked over the festive backyard shadowed by the fading sun.

"Possibilities... risks...," Kate whispered.

But no guarantees, Jess thought. And that was the part she was stuck on.

Kate bumped her hip against Jess. "The band will be starting soon. You go on now and enjoy your night."

The sun faded. Lawn torches were lit and the night air filled with six string entertainment provided by two brothers who lived on the island. Their guitars dueled, as they sung an eclectic selection of classic rock, country, and even a little blue grass for the old-timers. The chill of the island evening crept across the soft grass bringing a hint of fog. Riley climbed into Jess's lap and snuggled into the warmth of her body. "Ready to head out, bud?" She kissed his temple.

"Not tired," he yawned hugely.

Murphy was locked in a vicious contest, once again, with Rudy at the horseshoe pit. He'd been watching Jess between throws, as she smiled openly, enjoying the music. He'd seen her gather Riley with heavy eyelids onto her lap.

"Pay attention cowboy, you're about to go down," Rudy taunted.

Murphy stepped to the line, casually swung his long arm back, and tossed the horseshoe. The shoe hit with a clang, spiraling rapidly around the steel peg until it hit the soft sandy pit. "Going nowhere, old man," Murphy grinned into Rudy's weathered face. The men surrounding the pit howled with laughter. Murphy glanced again to where Jess and Riley had been seated and found her chair empty. His eyes scanned the yard just in time to glimpse her disappearing around the corner of the firehouse.

Jess jiggled her tote higher on her shoulder while she balanced the plate of leftovers Kate had insisted she take home. Riley leaned heavily against her side, threatening her center of gravity. "Few more steps, buddy. If you'd stop growing, I'd still be able to carry you."

"Hey Jess," Murphy jogged to catch up, "let me give you a hand." He hooked Riley around the waist and before Jess could think up a sensible reason to stop him, lifted him into the air. "Here we go big guy," Murphy smiled easily at Jess, "You guys going home? Want me to take your tote?"

"Yes, we are going home and no, I've got it thanks." Jess frowned as Riley settled effortlessly into Murphy's strong arms.

She was so used to operating on her own, but with Riley's cheek pressed against Murphy's shoulder, she softened. "You are going to forfeit your game."

"Sean stepped in for me."

"Then you lose for sure," she grinned. "Have you seen Sean play?"

"It's alright. I wouldn't want Rudy to lose his title. Besides," Murphy shrugged, "Sean's working on impressing Zoe."

"Match-making Murphy?" Jess pulled open the passenger door, "In you go buddy, and buckle up."

Murphy transferred Riley's exhausted form to the seat and whispered, "Thanks for helping me with the crabs. I'll see you later."

"When later?" His sleepy eyes fixed on Murphy's. "Are you herding tomorrow?"

"Sure am."

"Can I go with you?" Riley perked up.

"Well...I..."

"Nice try, little mouse," Jess intervened, when Murphy stuttered. "He's been trying all month to find someone to take him out herding."

"Oh momma," Riley whined, "I almost had him."

"Buckle up." Jess repeated, and closed the door.

"Has he ever ridden?"

"Sure, Sean takes him over to his parents' place. They have five ponies there. It's become a tradition in Sean's family to buy a pony from the auction. Sean tries to buy one every other year.

That's been one of Riley's determined ventures this year too, for us to buy a pony."

Murphy followed Jess to the driver's door. "Ponies are great for kids."

"Sure ponies are great for kids, if you have a place to care for them." Jess wagged her finger at him. "Oh no you don't. Don't gang up on me."

Murphy held his hands out innocently.

"Who wouldn't love a pony?" Jess rushed on. "It is just one of the many, many, things that are not in the realm of possibility for me." She tipped her head back and groaned. "Excuse the pity party. I am tired. Goodnight, Murphy."

He started to ask "what things", but the weariness in Jess's voice stopped him. "What are you doing tomorrow?"

"Work and date night, with my man, of course," Jess inclined her head at Riley who was fighting sleep. "Salty popcorn with too much butter, sci-fi movies with horrible special effects, and loaded ice cream sundaes..."

"Yum," Murphy grimaced.

"You'll be herding all day right?"

"Yep, and I've heard rumblings of a guys' night out."

"That sounds as scary as sci-fi and loaded sundaes." She climbed behind the wheel. "Have a safe ride Murphy and I'll see you around."

"Good night Jess, night Riley."

CHAPTER EIGHT

Murphy's lasso hung looped over the horn of his western saddle. Buzz tossed his head in the ocean breeze and sent his fringed mane rippling across his neck. It couldn't get much better than this, Murphy thought as he stood in the soft sand, amidst the sound of crashing waves, with an incredible horse beneath him. It had been a long day and the last herd had been a troublesome bunch. Murphy had worked a mare and her foal through the marsh, and back again, before he finally roped the mare and brought her alongside Buzz. The foal followed along closely, more frightened of being separated from his mother than moving beside a strange horse.

With the herd secured in the viewing corral, Murphy tied Buzz and walked along the tall fence. Vacationers crammed into the grassy area surrounding the enclosure. Camera shutters clicked rapidly capturing images of the wild ponies. Murphy moved to the far end of the corral to check on his favorite foal, the paint. The little paint's ears perked as Murphy drew near. Murphy propped his boot on the bottom wrung of the fence and studied the young one.

"Getting a crush?" Rudy said as he joined Murphy. "Make a nice addition for you back west."

"He's something, but I don't think I can check him in on the flight."

"Yeah that'd be something to see." Rudy opened his pouch of tobacco and loaded his cheek. "Plan on takin' any money home with you?"

Murphy raised his brow curiously.

"Poker, my boy, tonight at Sean's. I'll warn you the kid's a shark. You game?"

Murphy played with the guys on the ranch regularly, but he wasn't about to tip his hand. Also there was no mistaking the challenge in Rudy's tone. "Sounds good."

* * * *

The game was into its fifth hour and the pot was steep. Seated around the table were Rudy, Sean, Boots, Nub and Murphy. Rocco, Bobby and Andy had bowed out and watched the action from a safe distance as the sharks circled.

Rudy, cigar clamped between his teeth, examined his cards. He puffed three lazy rings of smoke and studied the faces around the table. The rings expanded as they floated into the hazy air. "Scoundrels," he said with disgust, and tossed his cards across the table. "I'm out." Rudy growled as he pushed his chair back and walked to the cooler for a fresh beer. The four remaining men duked it out for an additional hour until Sean painstakingly picked them off one by one.

"We going again?" Sean asked as he gathered the rich pot.

"Can't afford you, Boy," Rudy said.

"I'd rather spend my bucks at the Inn," Boots pulled on his jacket.

"I'm going home," Bobby said.

"Zoe's tending bar until midnight," Sean stated confidently. "Tonight's my night."

The men were all over him like mosquitoes in the marsh at sunset. Murphy shook his head. The kid needed to learn some things should be kept to himself.

"You in Murphy?" Rudy asked. "Good music, good company…"

"Hot women," Boots added with a cheesy grin. "You seen Zoe yet, Murphy?"

Sean's eyes, dark and dangerous, zipped to Murphy.

Murphy smirked, playing along. It was plain to see the kid had it bad. "I've seen her. A little skinny for my taste," Murphy shrugged. "Could be she'd go for a real cowboy. I'd be willing to make an exception." Sean's fists clenched at his hips. Murphy tipped his beer to his lips, then tossed the empty bottle into the recycle can. "Some women just go for a cowboy, that's all I'm saying."

The men hooted as Sean launched toward Murphy taking the bait. "Down boy," Rudy hooked Sean effortlessly around the middle. "You just make it too damn easy."

CHAPTER NINE

At daybreak the Saltwater Cowboys were assembled around the viewing corral. Rudy stood on the bed of a pick-up truck and issued the instructions for the day. "This is loose ends day, men. The sooner we pull the strings together, the sooner we are toasting our success and watchin' fireworks. I've posted assignments on the trailer and given each team leader a two-way radio to stay in touch." Rudy paused to slurp down some coffee. "So… we got strays to wrangle, final health check, branding, some general house keeping, corral maintenance and so on. Watch your language around the vacationers. Be sure to keep in mind that however annoying it might be having our island invaded, these people's cash make our world spin round and round."

Murphy stood next to Sean as Rudy's speech continued. "Oh…" Sean yawned, "Every year with the *dollars makes our world spin* shit. Could he be any more unoriginal?"

"Language Sean," Murphy snickered. "You wake up in the wrong bunk?"

Sean scrubbed his hand across his face, "Had a late night." There was no mistaking the pleasure in his tone.

Murphy took a good look at Sean. "Zoe?"

"Yeah," he answered dreamily. "Oh, not the way you're thinking." Sean's face flushed brightly.

"I wasn't thinking anything," Murphy held his palms out in defense.

73

"She's a good girl, woman," Sean amended. "Lord, if she doesn't twist me up. I watch the guys in the bar flirt with her. She's gorgeous no question, but I *know* her." Sean shrugged, "Zoe's got a lot going for her. I'm just not sure that I'm what she's after for the long haul, you know?"

"Hmm," Murphy studied Sean's serious face. He certainly admired his conviction. "Just remember all women, no matter what their age, want to be made to feel special. Any oaf could take Zoe out and drool over her."

Boots and Gus wandered toward the corral. Boots lightly nipped his fist on the back of Sean's shoulder. "Well big guy, you score?"

"What?" Sean said.

"Zoe? Slam dunk or what?" Boots made a dribbling motion and mocked shooting a basketball through a hoop.

"You're such a moron, Boots." Sean snapped.

"Told ya," Boots held out his hand and Gus slapped a ten dollar bill into his palm.

"You bet? You bet that I'd take her to bed?" Sean squawked.

"Thought you had it in you," Gus said simply. "No offense."

Sean looked at the pair of them with disgust, "I'm going to check the duty assignments. Coming Murphy?"

"Yep," Murphy strolled after Sean. "Shake it off buddy, small minds. No one's business but yours and Zoe's."

"Why do they have to cheapen' everything?" Sean stopped abruptly, and kicked the sand.

"Probably jealous."

"What?"

"I've only been here a week, but face it, Zoe has known all of you for years, right?" Sean nodded. "My take is if she was interested in cheap and casual, those bozos would have been with her by now. The way I see it, Zoe's a classy girl who might just have designs on a bigger prize."

Sean considered, "You may be right...I am a prize."

Murphy slapped Sean on the back, "That a boy."

Murphy and Sean had been paired with Bobby and Nub. They were two hours into the pursuit of strays. The marsh was unforgiving and the heat of the day was beginning to punch up. "There are no ponies out here," Sean called to Nub.

"Work the line and stop whining, Princess." Nub shouted back. "We've got about six hundred acres yet, and watch the sand for nests, all of you. Jess will skin us where we stand if we trample her eggs." The two-way buzzed at Nub's hip. "Yeah Chief."

Rudy's voice crackled over the line. "Boots and Gus found the last herd, bring it in."

"Rodger that." Nub shouted to his men, "We're done, Ladies. Let's head back."

It was mid-afternoon when Murphy and Sean leaned on the corral fence watching as the vet performed final evaluations on the ponies.

"You picked one yet?" Murphy asked Sean.

"Got my eye on a few," Sean smiled sheepishly. "Learned my lesson about telling anyone which foal specifically. Few years back Boots and Bobby bid against me for fun. Problem was no one let me in on the joke. Paid three hundred more than I should have."

"Ouch, hard lesson. Pretty cool your family's tradition of owning some."

"Soon we'll need to buy some more property. I never get tired of seeing young ones grow. They are so gentle and train easy. Everyone in my family cut their teeth riding Chincoteague ponies and they make great pasture buddies."

"Sean!" Riley raced across the grass. "Hey Murphy, you guys done herding?"

"Yep," Sean scooped Riley up in a swinging hug. "Where's your Momma?"

"She was late, so she dumped me." Riley shrugged, "She told me to tell you she's at the wildlife loop, her cell is on, and she shouldn't be more than an hour."

"No sweat, Buddy. What do you want to do for an hour?"

"I wanted to ride your horse," Riley's lip hung impressively. "I guess I am too late for that."

"Well...I did leave him saddled," Sean said casually, "and I just happened to park my trailer in the front lot."

"No foolin'?" Riley wiggled excitedly.

"No fooling, but before we go, I need your help." Sean turned and positioned Riley on the slats of the fence. "Since this isn't your year to have a foal of your own, I thought you could help me out. I need to you to pick your favorites but you have to keep them secret."

"I can keep a secret," Riley said sincerely.

"Study them, and we'll see if your favorites match up with mine."

"Cool."

Sean smiled over at Murphy. "Jess does a nature talk each week. This week she's doubled her schedule because of the penning crowd. Riley, what is your Mom's talk about today?"

"How would I know? I'm here." Riley rolled his eyes.

Sean swept him off the fence and tickled him, "Birds, turtles, little smart mouthed brats..."

Riley wriggled, "I'm no brat! Stop, stop," he squealed happily.

Sean settled Riley back on the fence, "Pick."

Murphy shook his head, "He's a handful."

"He's great. I hope to have about a dozen just like him. You going to the fireworks tonight, Murphy?"

"I guess... it's tradition right?"

"Yes, it's tradition," Riley leaned back holding the fence rail by the tiniest tips of his fingers. "Momma and I sit by the corral. She put the blanket down this morning to save our spot. You guys can sit with us if you want to."

"Not this year, I've got a hot date," Sean wiggled his brows.

"A date?" Riley wrinkled his nose. "Why would you want to have a hot date?"

"Why wouldn't I, is more the question. You'll understand when you are older."

"People always say that when they don't want to explain stuff to a kid," Riley huffed.

"Which foals do you like, Riley?" Murphy changed the subject.

Riley glanced around, and lowered his voice. "My number one favorite is the…"

Sean and Murphy listened to Riley's list. The boy had a good eye, Murphy realized. Sean and Riley conspired quietly and settled on a top five 'secret list' of foals. "Tell no one," Sean held out his hand to Riley to seal the deal.

Riley spat in his palm, "This is how you do it for real."

"Yuk," Sean pretended to gag.

"Come on Sean, don't be such a flower," Riley sounded like one of the guys at the station. "Spit or blood, I was trying to take it easy on you."

Murphy laughed as Sean spat into his palm and solemnly shook Riley's hand.

Rudy, Nub, Bobby and Boots strolled over to the corral. "Serious business happenin' here," Rudy noted the handshake.

Sean turned and stuffed his hands in his pockets. He knew what this group was up to. Riley mirrored him and then thrust his chin cockily in the air.

"You pick one out yet Sean?" Boots elbowed Nub.

"Maybe," Sean said smugly.

Boots kneeled in front of Riley, "I'll give you a twenty if you spill which pretty young thing he's after."

"Where's the money?" Riley said.

"Riley," Sean's shocked whisper etched out.

Riley ignored him and snatched the crisp twenty from Boots' fingers and jammed it deep into his jeans. Smelling victory, Boots grinned wickedly into Sean's face as he stood up.

"Well?" Boots straightened, "Which one does he want?"

Riley slowly looked at each of the men. Their interest peaked to the maximum. "Well..." Riley drawled, "Zoe of course. Thanks for the twenty, Boots."

Rudy's laughter roared from deep in his belly. "Got you good!" Rudy slapped Boots on the shoulder, and then he scooped Riley into his arms. "Damn boy, you make me proud."

CHAPTER TEN

Murphy followed Riley as he scampered along the nature trail. A canopy of Loblolly pines towered overhead masking the afternoon sun. They came upon a clearing where a group of people listened as Jess explained the management of the natural resources within the mudflats behind her. "As the spring rain falls, it floods areas like these and creates a perfect habitat for the migratory birds that visit our island throughout the summer."

Riley rushed ahead and slid on a bench at the rear of the group. Not wanting to disturb her presentation, Murphy leaned casually against a large tree. Jess spoke for about ten more minutes and then answered specific questions from the folks who hung behind. Murphy listened as she chatted with a couple dressed directly from the pages of a bird watcher apparel catalog; hats with wide brims and bug netting, binoculars and cameras strung around their necks and a pocket guide of the birds of the marsh. Jess was patient and incredibly knowledgeable. Finally the last couple moved off and Jess started to gather her instructional materials.

Riley ran over and wrapped his arms around her legs. "Momma, I got to ride Sean's horse all by myself."

"You did?"

"I rode all the way to the front parking lot. It was awesome. And I got to help Sean make a secret top five foal list and I invited him to the fireworks, but he has a hot date."

Jess's head whirled with her little man's excitement. "Take a breath, buddy. I hope you thanked Sean. Where is he?" She turned and found Murphy smiling at her from against the tree. Good gracious, a mere glance of the man was lethal. Her pulse hammered so loudly in her head she couldn't hear herself think. "How did you get stuck with Riley? I hope he wasn't any trouble. When did you slip in? I was so wrapped up in the talk I didn't see you guys. Were you waiting long?"

She was awfully cute when she was flustered. Murphy straightened and moved toward her. "Not long, can I give you a hand?"

"I got it, thanks." Jess snapped her case closed and slung it over her shoulder. Murphy stood beside her, his thumbs hooked casually through his belt loops. As he studied her, the butterflies in her belly jumped to life. He was a fantasy man and her dormant hormones had little restraint. Jess took a slow breath and attempted to settle her thundering heart. "How was herding? All the ponies accounted for?"

"Yep, I guess now I have a few days off until the swim."

"You need to work on checking off that list of yours, Murphy."

"The guys are taking me out bay fishing tomorrow."

"That's a start," Jess laughed. "Whose boat are you in?"

"Rudy's... is that a good choice?"

"Yeah, you should be safe."

"Come on Momma, I want to go home." Riley sat on the bench, legs swinging.

"I'm coming, Sweetie." Jess smiled wearily at Murphy. "It's been a long day for everyone and it's not over yet, fireworks tonight at the fairgrounds."

He could see the fatigue hiding in her eyes. "Can you grab some down-time before?"

"That's my plan. Are you planning to go tonight?"

"Murphy doesn't have a hot date, like Sean, so he's free." Riley stretched across the bench on his belly and pretended to swim the breaststroke.

Jess released an exasperated sigh, "Riley, let's get going." Jess eased him off the bench. "Give you a lift, Murphy?"

"Only if I can ask you a question."

Jess could see that gleam of mischief in his smile. "What question would that be?"

"Wanna' be my hot date to the fireworks?"

"Hot dates…" Riley groaned, "Grown ups are disgusting."

CHAPTER ELEVEN

Reclining on a soft quilt, Murphy, Jess, and Riley looked into the sky as another blast of color erupted. "Wow, that one was the best," Riley commented.

"You've said that about each and every one," Jess giggled.

"I think he's right," Murphy bumped Riley, "That one was the best."

The next set was a triple. Vibrant colors intermingled and then were punctuated by three deafening booms! Riley pulled the quilt over his head. "Hate those."

"Me too," Jess shivered.

Murphy laughed at the two of them hiding like frightened cats. Why was it he wanted to wrap his arms around the pair of them and hold on? It just didn't make any sense.

Across the lawn Kate leaned against the refreshment booth. She had stopped looking at the sky fifteen minutes ago, when Jess's laugh had floated through the evening air. The delightful sound had Kate seeking Jess out within the crowd, and when her eyes settled upon her ...well, oh my. The sight of Murphy and Jess book ending Riley on the blanket had caused Kate's heart to simply melt. Girls would be girls no matter their age, after all. They looked like a family. Any stranger to the island would assume as much. Kate wondered if Jess knew the joy radiating from her was as luminous as the colors that streaked across the night sky. Kate only hoped that when the sparks of this particular firework faded, Jess would still be in one piece.

"What you staring at, Katie?" Rudy slid beside Kate along the wall.

"Nothing. What are you up to?" Kate turned and blocked Rudy's sight line. She knew Rudy had an overprotective tendency when it came to Jess and Riley. "How did your ride go today?"

Rudy studied Kate's forced smile and overly friendly nature. The woman was up to no good. He nimbly picked her up and set her aside.

Kate's already light heart fluttered as Rudy lifted her as if she weighed nothing. She barely had a moment to catch her breath when she heard him growl.

"I'll take care of this right now."

"Oh no you don't," Kate snagged his arm. "Settle a moment. Hey." She pulled his arm firmly when he resisted. "You need to let her have a little rope."

"She'll be hangin' in the wind. Look at him, all snuggled up with them like he owns 'em," Rudy bristled.

"I've done little but look at them for the last few minutes. It's a beautiful thing to watch hearts trip over one another."

Rudy studied Murphy carefully. He was relaxed, leaning back on his hands with his legs stretched across the blanket. Riley was burrowed into Jess's side peeking from under the blanket while she held his ears. Rudy huffed. He figured it might be okay, but he didn't care for the way the locals were noticing them. More than a few people had their eyes focused on Jess and the Cowboy, and not the display in the sky.

"She deserves a little time to feel like a woman, Rudy. It will be all right."

Rudy turned and looked into Kate's glowing face. "I guess Jess can handle herself. Murphy will be leaving in a few days anyway. But... you better buy some ice cream, Katie. Isn't that what you girls do after your hearts get smashed?"

Kate softened. "Surly one minute, kindhearted the next. You're a good man Rudy, you know that?"

Rudy smiled down into Kate's face as the fireworks reflected in her eyes. A ghost of a smile teased his lips, "Don't let it get around."

CHAPTER TWELVE

Murphy walked into the fire hall as instructed at just before 5:00 A.M. He was certain Rudy expected him to flinch at the hour, but getting up at sunrise was not a habit that got broken after a few days at the beach. Music was coming from the weight room, so Murphy headed that way. Sean was working with dumbbells while Boots, Nub, and Bobby stood watching.

"So you ditched us for a chick and won't even give us a single detail?" Boots poked Sean's chest. "Aww Puny, did she turn you down? Is your ego bruised this morning?"

Here we go again, Murphy thought, poor Sean.

"Leave him be, maybe he's just respecting the lady." Nub said.

"He didn't get anywhere...*again*." Boots shook his head. "How about you Cowboy, you finding any luck with our Nature Girl? I saw the two of you snuggled up at the fireworks. Ro-man-tic." Boots batted his eyes, drawing a few snickers from the group.

Sean placed the dumbbells on the rack. "Knock it off," he smacked Boots in the shoulder.

"Calm down Puny, I just figured she might play for the other side."

"Just because Jess has enough sense not to look at you twice doesn't mean she's gay," Sean said angrily.

"Not just me, no one. She didn't look at you either kid, or Nub, or even Rudy, for pity sake. I'm just saying I figured it could be men all together, but she's got the kid so..." Boots ignored the warning looks from his buddies and continued to flap his lips. "...she's making time for the Cowboy isn't she?" Boots looked at Murphy. "Maybe Murphy would like to put this little mystery to rest."

Murphy's body tensed with fury, the muscles jumped along his jaw as he took two slow purposeful strides toward Boots.

"Enough." Rudy snapped abruptly, then turned his heated gaze to Boots.

It gave Murphy a little satisfaction to watch him squirm. He just wished Rudy hadn't beaten him to the punch.

"None of my business, Murphy," Boots swallowed hard, "my apologies."

Murphy nodded curtly.

"Don't you 'knuckle noodles' have gear to load?"

"Yes chief," Sean and Boots hurried from the room.

Rudy's back was ramrod straight as he glared at Murphy. "Let's get going." Murphy followed Rudy into the kitchen. Without a word, Rudy filled two travel mugs with coffee, handed one to Murphy, nodded at a pile of fishing gear on the counter, grabbed a small cooler, and walked out the back door. Murphy picked up a backpack and joined Rudy in the truck.

They were several blocks away before Rudy spoke. "This is gonna' roll off my tongue all wrong, but it needs sayin'." Murphy tipped his head in acknowledgment. "Jess is the daughter I didn't take the time to create. She's special. That boy of hers is special. They're the kind of special that can't stand up against mean or stupid town talk. They are the kind of special that deserves special in return. The people who should have stood with her when Riley came along didn't. She has made a life for him here, on her own. She built it. Although she presents an iron will, it wouldn't take a hurricane to shake her up." Rudy paused long enough to sip his coffee. "Now, you don't impress me as a careless man, Murphy, but your life is a half a country away from this little island. I don't see what your intentions could be. My Jess is too special for casual."

Murphy allowed Rudy to talk. He'd been thinking the same thing all along. But there was just something about Jess that pulled at him. When Rudy's next pause became a break, Murphy spoke. "Jess and I've been straight with each other from the day we met, Rudy. We have our eyes wide and we have no intention of hurting each other."

"Intention has little to do with it." Rudy filled his lungs and prepared to start again.

"I'm not brushing you off Rudy." Murphy looked Jess's honorary father square in the eyes. "I heard everything you said."

"Good." Rudy said briskly, and then exhaled slowly. "Good...now, then let's get these 'knuckle noodles' in the boat and get fishin'."

The men hustled to load the boat and within the hour were floating in the bay with the morning sun lighting their faces.

Rudy wrapped a piece of cut squid around a hook and handed it to Murphy. "We've got about ten feet of water here. Let out enough line so the bait bounces on the bottom." Other vessels dotted the bay. Engines off, the boats drifted soundlessly in the constantly shifting water. Time after time, the tide would carry the boats out of position and Captains would simply fire the motors and pull the small crafts back into place.

The boat rocked gently as the tide shifted beneath it. "Look there," Rudy pointed across the water. Dolphins broke the surface about forty yards from their boat. "Doin' some herdin' of their own."

Murphy watched as the dolphins splashed and jumped, working together to move a school of·fish into a tight group for easier feeding. At one point the huge ocean mammals leapt fully out of the water. "Incredible," Murphy said ignoring his rod which bowed into the water.

"You gonna' pull that in?" Sean called to Murphy.

"No, he'd rather let it swim around with a hook speared through its lip and tell all its underwater buddies not to eat the squid." Boots said flippantly.

Murphy reeled the line in and a spiky fish about eight inches long wiggled on the end. He reached out and grabbed the fish, which responded with a *Grooak.*

"What the hell!" Murphy let the fish swing away from him.

"Grab it Boy!" Rudy and the men laughed. "It's a croaker. Good eatin'."

Murphy studied the dangling fish. *Grooak, grooak,* it said again. "That is the damndest thing." Murphy gripped the croaking fish and extracted the hook from his lip.

"Toss it in the ice chest, boy," Rudy said. "Then bait up, we'll eat good tonight."

The men fished the bay until the cooler was full and their bellies were rumbling.

Rudy guided the boat into the marina. Sean hopped out and secured the lines to the dock. With admirable efficiency, the catch transferred to the truck, the gear was washed down, and the boat hosed out. In record time the men were on their way headed back to the firehouse for a fish fry feast.

CHAPTER THIRTEEN

The fish fry rolled over into a guys' night at the Inn. Murphy stood with the bay breeze rushing into his face. Overhead stars winked and the moon shown bright against the dark cloudless sky. Another local band was providing tonight's entertainment. The atmosphere on the deck was the same island casual it had been every time Murphy had been here.

"Come on Murphy, you're fallin' behind." Sean's youthful face was flushed. He handed Murphy a cold beer. "You see Zoe? If she ain't the prettiest thing on the planet."

"You talk to her tonight?"

"Yep, we seem to have us an understanding," Sean lifted his hand and grinned.

Murphy looked over at the bar. Zoe's cheeks were bright pink as she smiled at Sean. "You hanging 'til she's off work?"

"Not tonight, she has plans with her girlfriends." Sean raised his shoulder. "I'm trying not to crowd her. What I want to do is carry her off somewhere private for the next hundred years."

Murphy laughed, "Better stick to your first plan and give her a little space."

"Yeah, I know, but I don't have to like it." Sean tipped his beer. "One day until the pony swim. What are you planning on doing tomorrow?"

Murphy shrugged, "Got nothing firm."

"The guys and I are taking the jet skis and hitting the inlet for some kite boarding and windsurfing. Man day. You up for it?"

Murphy had stopped hearing Sean the second Jess had moved into the room. She was still in her work clothes and she looked exhausted. Riley scooted around her and jumped up on a stool overlooking the bay. Carrying a soda and a tall glass of water, Jess moved to the table and melted into a chair beside Riley. "Murphy?" Sean nudged him. "You've got other plans for tomorrow, like maybe with a certain foxy nature girl?"

"Huh?" Murphy shifted his attention back to Sean. "No, no. I'm not sure what I'm doing tomorrow." As much as he wanted to spend the day with Jess, he was going to try to put some distance there. Rudy was right, she and Riley deserved more than he could offer.

"Well the guys want to try to get their money back from me. So we are heading back to my place for a poker rematch. You want in?"

Murphy looked over the water. Anywhere he didn't have to look at Jess would be better than trying to ignore her. "Yeah, poker suits me."

Sean rubbed his hands together, "Prepare to lose some bucks Murphy. I'm on a hot streak."

While Kate placed Jess and Riley's dinner order, she became aware of Murphy trying not to notice Jess. "Fickle man," she muttered. The firefighters started to clear their tabs and move along for the night. Sean and Zoe were having a hushed conversation at the end of the bar. Kate overheard Sean as he told Zoe he was going to clean up at poker. Kate watched the youngsters as they whispered quietly to one another while their fingers twined together behind the bar out of sight from the other patrons. Young love. Kate's heart twittered. "Hey Zoe, why don't you take your break," Kate moved behind the bar. "I'll settle these guys' tabs. Sean, you square?"

"Yes'mm."

Kate moved Zoe along with a whisper, "Take a minute and say goodbye to your man properly."

Zoe's cheeks flushed with color, but she hooked Sean's arm and pulled him out the side door, away from interested eyes and ears.

"You meddlin' Katie?" Rudy eyed her over the rim of his glass.

"So what if I am old man? No business of yours."

Rudy grunted as Kate moved down the bar, and then shifted his attention across the room to Murphy. He'd seen the heat in Murphy's gaze when Jess had walked into the Inn. Rudy planned to camp out, right here on the bar stool, until he was certain his little chat with Murphy had made the impression it needed to.

Jess carried her empty water glass to the bar for a refill. She glanced over at Murphy leaning easily against the deck rail. "Hey Murphy, how's your day treating you?"

"Good," Murphy smiled.

"You guys go fishing?"

"Yep, we had a good day." Murphy rooted his boots to the floor. He itched to join Jess and Riley at the table and hear all about their day. He also knew it was just the type of casual gesture he should avoid. The muscle in Murphy's jaw tensed, as he caught the steely look from Rudy three stools down. Murphy shoved the desire to chat with Jess aside and stepped to the bar. "Kate, would you get my bill please?"

"You headin' out Handsome?"

95

"Yep, serious poker," Murphy handed Kate a twenty. "Keep the change, see you guys later."

Kate and Jess watched as Murphy left the bar without explanation. "What was that about?" Jess asked Kate. "Do I stink?" Despite her light tone the hurt was crystal clear in her eyes. Jess bit her lip, lifted her water from the bar and returned to the table.

Kate closed the cash register and heard Rudy as he muttered into his glass, "Good man."

"Good man what?" She moved in front of Rudy and scowled at his arrogant expression. "What have you done?"

"What are you fussin' about now?" Rudy wouldn't meet her eyes.

Kate slapped her palm on the bar. "What have you done?"

"Nothin'," Rudy said innocently.

Kate leaned across the bar, "Spill it, Rudy."

"I just explained to Murphy that Jess and Riley were not the casual type," his temper clipped. "I told him to put some distance there, that's all."

"Stupid man...stupid, stupid man." Kate took Rudy's glass and emptied the contents. "Pay up, you old goat."

"Hey, I wasn't done with that."

"Oh, you're done. Pay your tab and get."

Rudy tossed the bills on the counter and headed across the scarred planks. "Women don't have the sense to know when someone's trying to help them out."

Jess sipped her water as she mentally berated herself for her idiocy. She had known better than to get carried away with a crush. For heavens sake, she barely knew the man. Reality was what worked for her and reality was seated three feet across the table from her right now. "What you seeing out there, little man?"

Riley scanned the dark bay, and relayed the simplicity captured through his innocent eyes. He described the moon's reflection, the sleepy birds, the slap of the water along the dock... each word he muttered healed his momma's wounded heart.

Kate snatched a bottle of ketchup for Riley's fries and moved purposely to the table. "Here we go. Riley. Your fries are really hot, so be careful, you hear?" Kate placed her hands on Jess's shoulders and began to rub gently. "Jessie girl, this crab cake looked so good I ordered one myself. Mind if I join you?"

Jess smiled up at Kate. "That would be perfect." She picked up a chip.

"Don't wait on me. You eat that sandwich while it's hot. You need the fuel." Kate squeezed the ketchup onto Riley's plate. "Mine will be along in a minute." Jess laid her hand palm up on the table. Kate clasped it tightly and the understanding passed between the women.

"Could I have been more foolish?" Jess asked quietly.

"Foolish just left the bar, and I'm not talking about Handsome, although he runs a close second." Jess blinked at Kate, obviously confused. Kate patted her hand, "Eat and I'll explain the brainless, backward, nature of men, compounded by..." Kate covered Riley's ears before adding, "Their innate stupidity."

CHAPTER FOURTEEN

Fists pounded on the door and rebounded inside Murphy's skull like racket balls. He'd kill Sean when he got close enough to grasp his scrawny neck. He had no intention of windsurfing with the scoundrel who had taken his money twice in one week. Losing his money had done nothing to improve his sour mood after running out on Jess at the Inn.

The rapping grew more insistent. "I'm coming, you knuckle noodle." Murphy's bare feet slapped the ceramic tile. "If you value your young life, you'll quit hammering on the damn door." He whipped open the door, fully prepared to chew Sean a new hind end. Murphy pulled up short and artfully swallowed the curse on the tip of his tongue. It was Jess who stood before him, not Sean. He stared blankly at her for a full ten seconds and then scrubbed his hand across his face. "Jess," he said flatly.

"Murphy." Jess said seriously, then laughed as she held out a cup of coffee. Murphy muttered a thank you and gratefully sucked down the coffee like a dying man.

Think, think, think... Murphy willed his brain to wake up. He'd decided last night that as long as he didn't see her, he could break this hold she seemed to have on him.

Now, Jess stood before him fresh faced, hair threaded through the back of a ball cap, offering him coffee. The sight of her destroyed his resolve to keep his distance. "What are you doing here Jess?"

"Playing hooky, which is a first for me," she tipped her head and smiled brightly into his stern face. "I'm shanghaiing you Murphy."

Wishing for a dimmer switch for the wattage beaming from her grin, Murphy cowardly focused on the chilly ceramic beneath his feet. "I don't think that's a good idea, Jess."

Her confidence wavered. Maybe she shouldn't have listened to Kate's pep talk. Maybe bold was a bad move. *'All or nothing Jessie girl'*, Kate's words flooded Jess's mind. *'Go after what you want in life or forever face regret.'* Jess squared her shoulders, took a deep breath, "I just want the day, Murphy. One day. Could we pretend life is simple for one day? Let's mark off some of that list of yours. I've got kayaks, surf fishing gear, a picnic lunch...Come play with me Murphy."

It was just what he wanted and knowing he should refuse, slam the door and hide from all the feelings she stirred in him, wasn't enough. He was a millisecond from falling into a pit he knew he'd never crawl from. He could offer her nothing. She deserved everything. *'Special'*, Rudy had said, *'Not casual.'*

"Jess..." Murphy shook his head "I can't. It's just that..." he started to form a lie to let her down easy.

"Murphy listen to me, please. I know Rudy warned you off. I know I'm a mother with responsibilities and I know you have a life a world away from here. But I also know life changes in an instant. I just want today." Her eyes pleaded and the crater formed beneath his feet.

Murphy leaned against the door frame and studied her. "First off, Riley has nothing to do with this. He's a great kid and you are a terrific mother. Okay?"

"Okay."

Murphy lifted the coffee and slipped slowly, buying a few more seconds. As he lowered the cup, Jess was treated to one of his killer smiles. "We are going to need some rules."

Jess relaxed at his playful change of demeanor. "You set them this time."

"Alright...I'll go with you, because I want to. I'll surf fish and kayak, because I'm dying to try it, and I respect your integrity, so I won't be sleeping with you."

She laughed and poked him in the chest. "Get dressed Cowboy, the day's a-wasting."

Jess drove to the northern parking lot on Assateague, eased the Jeep to the shoulder, and set the brake. "We need to release the air pressure in the tires to have traction in the sand." She hopped out of the Jeep and tossed Murphy two tiny clamps. "Secure these on the valve stems on your side." Jess leaned down to the front tire. "Like this. Got it?"

"Yeah," Murphy did as instructed.

"When I tell you, pull them off and then I'll check the pressure." A few moments later, they cruised across the open sand. Since an off-road permit was required to drive on the beach, only the diehard fishermen and locals inhabited this remote part of the island. Jess drove for nearly three miles before backing the Jeep into the shoreline, being certain to stay far enough from the water to allow for the changing tide.

"Surf fishing first," Jess said.

Standing in the break Murphy held the heavy rod and reel. The powerful undertow pulled the bait toward the sea. "How will I know when I have a hit?" Murphy called to Jess over the sound of the rushing waves.

"You'll know." Jess answered. Murphy looked down the beach where fishermen worked their lines. Some held their rods, others sat in chairs with their rods resting in PVC tubes anchored in the firm sand. Occasionally one of the men would get lucky and drag a flopping fish onshore. He and Jess had been at it more than an hour and so far had done nothing but feed the fish.

"Humph," Murphy shrugged. Surf fishing was not as easy as he'd figured.

"Had enough?" Jess called.

"I hate to fail at anything, but if I'm going to be honest, that kayak has peaked my curiosity."

Jess grinned, "Let's do it!"

They stowed the fishing gear and lifted the kayak from the Jeep's roof rack. It was a two seated, hard plastic, buoyant craft, nearly ten feet in length. Jess reached behind the Jeep's seat and pulled out two life jackets, two paddles, sun block, spandex cords, and strings with small metal fasteners on each end.

"Necessary," Jess said as she tossed him a life jacket.

"Encouraging," Murphy grimaced. "What's the other stuff?"

"This," she held out the spandex, "will hold your sunglasses on your face. This," she held out the cord with clamps, "will keep your hat on your head, and this," she wagged the sun block at him, "will keep your skin on your bones."

With all of their protective gear in place, Murphy and Jess dragged the kayak through the sand and surf, and walked into the ocean. Waist deep with the kayak between them, Jess told Murphy to climb on. He pressed his palms firmly on the plastic, testing the stability. On the next swell, he lifted himself from the water, mounting the boat as easily as he would his horse, leaving his long legs dangling over the sides.

"Legs up Cowboy," Jess tapped his thigh. "When I get on, we'll need to move fast." The next wave rushed over the front of the boat, and Murphy felt certain he'd pitch over the side. Surprised he was still planted on the slippery seat, Murphy grinned. "Keep the front pointed west into the waves or we'll be dumped hard, and that's no way to start our adventure." Jess placed her palms flat and lithely hoisted her lean body onto the kayak. "Pull Murphy, PULL!" Jess dug her paddle into the whitecap as the next wave bared down on them. Smoothly they propelled the kayak through the swell and dropped into the trough behind it.

"Whew, that was…"

"Not done yet Murphy," Jess, all business, instructed urgently. "One more, DIG!" Murphy matched her strong arms and kept the boat pointed west as she had ordered. Once again they moved up an incline of powerful water and down the other side. "Now you may rest," Jess laughed. "You did pretty well for a westerner."

"That was incredible," Murphy said. "I'd hate to see what happened if we'd gotten caught by the water."

"It's not pretty, I promise you, but once you're out here it's worth it." Jess paddled keeping them facing the oncoming waves. They were beyond the break but she wasn't sure how Murphy would feel about tipping in the thirty-foot deep water. Above them a pelican tucked his wings and dove toward the surface. A moment later, with barely a whisper of sound, the bird's body disappeared into the blue water.

"Awesome." Murphy said. The kayak glided until they were forty yards off the beach. Murphy was amazed at the clear water. Beneath him fish swam and stingrays zipped. "Where were all of you when I was fishing?"

"Dining on your bait," Jess chuckled.

"I can't get over that they are right here, this close to the beach, with all that open water." Murphy gestured to the sea. "Less predators near the surf?"

"Smaller ones at least."

They drifted at the ocean's mercy. Every now and again Jess would look over to see how far the tide had shifted them and they would paddle the kayak back into position.

"You could float away in minutes," Murphy said. "I feel like we are sitting still, until I look at the vehicles on shore."

"Yes, that is one of the dangers if you are inexperienced. Lots of vacationers fail to respect the ocean's current and end up needing rescue." Jess scanned the waters' surface. "If there are fish, we could get lucky... Yes, there." she said excitedly, and pointed across the waves. Murphy looked over just as a school of dolphins broke the surface. "Let's go!" Murphy timed his paddle with hers as she pulled at the water and led them within yards of the active pod.

Entranced, Murphy watched the pod feeding. "They're bigger than you'd expect."

"Yeah," Jess heard the wonder in his voice, "Pretty great, huh."

The pod played and circled the school of fish for nearly an hour. Jess leaned back on her elbows, stretched her legs over the front of the kayak and watched the show. The power of nature could be beyond astounding.

The group moved off and Murphy glanced over at the beach. "Well, we've drifted a little far from home."

"Oops, sorry, stopped watching the shore." Jess sat up and dug her paddle in. "So much for irresponsible vacationers," Jess sulked. "We've got two options here Murphy. We paddle against tide or we beach it and walk the kayak back on shore."

"Let's split the distance." They dug the paddles in and worked their way toward the halfway point.

Jess turned the front of the boat toward the beach. "Now...getting out without dumping can be tricky."

"What shouldn't I do?"

"I admire that trait in you Murphy, always wanting a guide-line. It sounds simple; we need to keep the kayak pointed straight into the shore. The waves will shift unpredictably and change our angle." Jess peeked over her shoulder and observed Murphy's fierce expression. "We commit, we stay straight, and we'll beach and look like we know exactly what we're doing."

"Well. I'd sure hate to look like an idiot," Murphy said seriously, making Jess chuckle.

"Alright Murphy, match me." Jess paddled, then hesitated as the wave gathered beneath them. The water shifted and Murphy dragged his paddle and forced the boat to stay facing the shore. "Good," Jess said, "again."

They repeated the process three more times. Murphy was certain they still had one more wave to go until he realized they were sitting on a curl of white water. Jess and the front end of the craft jutted out from the wave unsupported. He only had a second to panic before the white water smashed across the sand. Despite the loud crash of water, the wave deposited them neatly in the sudsy surf. The kayak rode the rush of water before settling effortlessly on the wet sand as the water retreated to the sea.

"We're good." Jess said clapping her hands.

Exhilarated, Murphy grinned. "No sweat," he said, even as his tripping pulse mocked him.

* * * *

Stretched out in the cool shade of a striped umbrella, Murphy looked as content as a lazy cat. Kneeling beside him, Jess flipped open the cooler and started to pack up the remainders of lunch.

"Give me two minutes and I will help you," Murphy said without moving. Jess smiled down at him. His feet were crossed at the ankles, his hands behind his head, and his hat tipped down across his eyes. In another few minutes, he'd be snoring soundly.

When everything was cleaned up, Jess looked out across the water. In the distance, container ships and fishing vessels could be seen against the horizon. Jess's mind drifted as she watched them move through the sea. She loved to speculate and spin fanciful tales in her mind of the captains and crew. Where were they headed? What had they caught today? Did they have families who would race to the dock to see their catch?

Jess crawled soundlessly across the blanket and eased her hip to the blanket beside Murphy. His chest lifted and fell steadily as he slept. Poor guy. A night with the boys followed by sunrise fishing and kayaking had to be tough. She stared down at the man who had touched something in her in a matter of days. Strong physically, that was obvious, but the little he'd shared with her about his childhood had showed strength too. Solid family bonds; mother, sister, grandparents. Something she'd had once upon a time. Something she also knew could be lost in an instant. Jess shook off the sadness. She had ordered a perfect day and... she smiled down at Murphy, she'd have it.

She tucked herself next to him, rested her head on his chest, and listened to the ocean. Murphy shifted in his sleep and draped his arm across Jess's hip. She froze until she was certain he slept again. She knew she'd hold this moment for a lifetime; lying on the soft sand in the passing heat of the day with a strong man. Someday timing would be on her side and she'd have moments like this for longer than a few days.

Murphy stirred. He felt Jess against him and allowed the waves to continue to lull him. "Whoa, sorry Jess, I fell clean out, didn't I?"

"You sure did," Jess teased but snuggled against him. Murphy slid his arm slowly up to her waist and pulled her closer.

"How do you feel about a swim?" Jess asked.

"Wouldn't say no."

Jess sat up and looked at his hat covered face. Playfully she lifted the hat. "Wake up Cowboy." She tossed the hat aside and stripped her shirt over her head revealing her tankini. She stood and wriggled out of her shorts.

Murphy opened his eyes just enough to watch the show. Men would be men after all.

"Let's go Murphy."

Murphy boosted up on his elbows and watched Jess race into the surf never hesitating as the waves bore down on her. She dove into the towering water and surfaced on the other side. Murphy pulled his shirt over his head and tossed it on the blanket. He walked into the surf, wincing inwardly at the cold water against his heated skin. He tried to time the assault of the waves as he headed in. Jess laughed, when Murphy's eyes shot wide as the wave caught him. He braced as the wall of water slammed into him and stood up sputtering.

"Duck under!" Jess called.

Murphy heard her in the nick of time. He sucked in precious air and submerged. He surfaced next to Jess in the five foot deep water where she floated on her back, lazily kicking her feet. The water rolled over them. Beyond the break, they were in no danger of being flattened.

"The bottom is shelly," Murphy said.

"Um hmm," Jess answered. "If you feel around with her toes you may find a few that are nice sized. Just watch out for the occupied ones."

They floated side by side in the cool water. Easy, comfortable, perfect, Jess thought. "So what do you think, Murphy?" Can we mark off surf fishing and kayaking from your list?"

"Yes, but I've added a few more."

"Really?" Jess dipped her head back in the water.

"Floating with you, just like this."

Jess lifted her head and looked at him. His eyes closed, his body suspended on the gentle swells. "I'll agree to that." She treaded closer and held out her hand.

Murphy gazed over at her as she linked her fingers through his. "I know we're not going to sleep together but could I hold you and float a bit?"

Jess allowed Murphy to pull her in front of him. "I ordered a perfect day, and that sounds perfect to me." He spun her so her back was against his chest. Jess lifted her toes to the surface and kicked lightly. With his hands wrapped around her waist, they faced the horizon together.

When the moment shifted, Jess wasn't sure. She separated Murphy's hands and spun to her belly facing him. "I'm not a reckless or fanciful woman. There's a lot we don't know about each other."

Murphy watched her green eyes change, deepen. Mermaid eyes, he thought, eyes that seemed to gaze right through him.

"But in my perfect day…with you…without complications… our float includes a kiss."

Murphy held completely still. The next wave moved her body to his. Her hands slipped against his wet skin until they wrapped around his neck. "Would that be all right?" She whispered as she closed the distance.

It took great effort for Murphy to allow Jess to lead the moment. She wanted perfection and in Murphy's book, this was pretty damn close. As Jess eased back, her green eyes pierced his soul. Murphy studied her seriously. It was on the tip of his tongue to promise her the world; to scoop her and Riley up and make a life together in Montana. A life that was his not hers, they'd be doomed before they even began.

Jess wriggled uneasily under Murphy's scrutiny. Weren't men into the "no strings" kind of thing? It had been some time since she played this game. She smiled, determined to move forward with her keep-it-light plan for the day. "Have enough water?" she asked. "How about we take a walk and dry off."

* * * *

It was after 2:00 when Murphy and Jess wandered back from their walk. Murphy spied something reflecting in the surf. "Did you see that flash?" he asked Jess.

"Where?"

"When the wave rolled in across the shells I saw a quick flash of color." Murphy pointed in to the frothy water. "Maybe my eyes are playing tricks."

Jess moved into the breaking waves and scooped up a handful of shells and sifted them slowly through her fingers. She explained how the agitation of the salt and sand combined with the force of the water gradually polished the broken shells. Artists combed the shoreline collecting the pieces to create mosaics, and jewelry. "Lately the trend has become beach glass. That's probably what you saw flash. Broken bottles get milled by the natural elements and lose their sharp edges. Green, white, blue, and amber. The glass can be hard to find."

"Does it look like this?"

Murphy held out an aqua green piece about one inch long. The smooth surface had been abraded to the point that the glass had begun to lose its shine and become cloudy.

"That's a great one. The cloudy color means it's been in the water a long time."

"Come here," Murphy held out his hand.

Jess reached across and latched on as the wave rushed past them. Murphy tucked the glass into her hand. Jess looked down at the beautifully polished fragment and then up at the man who handed it to her. Murphy leaned down and kissed her lightly, "To remember our perfect day."

CHAPTER FIFTEEN

Murphy stood at the double glass doors sipping iced tea as the sun sank into the west. With each minute that slipped past, the late afternoon sky shifted from perfect blue to tangerine and pink. Murphy had started to look forward to this part of the day. He watched a fisherman in a short aluminum boat check his crab pots. Motoring slowly through the water, the single man crew pulled up to a buoy and hauled up the trap from the choppy water. Laden with crabs, the fisherman emptied the 'keepers' into a basket, and tossed the small crabs back into the water. With precision, the wire trap was baited once again and dropped over the side of the boat. The fisherman motored the small craft to the next marked buoy. The process was slow, but systematic. Murphy appreciated the logical, efficient work plan.

Life at the seashore was working its magic on him, but it wasn't home. Murphy emptied the glass of sweet tea and glanced at the clock. "Good a time as any," he moved through the living room, placed his cup on the kitchen counter, and snagged the phone from the wall.

Tory picked up on the second ring. "Murphy?"

He laughed heartily at his sister, "Missing me Tory?"

"Yes, desperately," Tory giggled. "You want the sixty second update?"

"Give it to me."

"Well...Momma checked in. She and Ed are headed for St. Martin for some much needed tropical therapy. I told her you would be a beach pro after this trip, and maybe she should invite you to join them."

"It's growing on me... the beach."

"Well don't strap your sandals on quite yet dear brother. Your new mare is arriving in a few days and I have acquired another mouth to feed, a llama of all things. He's two years old and is a terrible flirt!"

Murphy knew his sister had a weakness for taking in strays. She had made quite a name for herself rescuing neglected and abused animals from around the state. She worked tirelessly to rehabilitate them and adopt them out to good homes. It was only one of her many passions. Murphy laughed, "What's his name, our resident llama gigolo?"

"Smooch!" Tory laughed. "Speaking of smooching, found anything of interest to occupy your time? Joel says the ladies of the seashore are always happy to make the cowboys welcome."

"Joel exaggerates, but yeah actually I had a day of adventure yesterday...," Murphy drifted off thinking of Jess.

Tory heard the subtle change in Murphy's voice. "Is everything okay?" They had always been more than siblings, and much more than friends. Theirs was a kinship that surpassed any defined relationship. "Murphy?" Tory said again when he didn't answer her.

"I think you were right... my heart hadn't ever been taken from me."

"Oh Murphy...tell me about her."

"It's complicated. It could never work, and this time, even though I had my eyes wide open..." he trailed off, "I don't know."

Tory's heart broke for him. She had no details but she knew, felt rather, the depth of Murphy's feelings without another word. "Start at the beginning and we'll figure it all out."

Murphy was exhausted by the time he hung up the phone. Tory had always been a champion listener. Murphy appreciated her insight but most of all it had helped him to allow it all to spill out of him. Hearing the words from his own mouth as he described Jess and Riley and the simple things they had shared together made him realize the truth in his feelings. It really didn't matter what direction he had thought his life was headed. Love was love; inconvenient, difficult, demanding, selfless, generous, fulfilling, but more than all that; love was a gift. A once in a lifetime gift which, given the opportunity, could be everything.

Murphy didn't know what that would mean for him by the end of this trip. What he did know, was that vacation was wearing him out. Who knew sun, surf, and fun could wear a man out equally as well as a hard day of ranching. He wandered through the quiet house flipping off the lights on the way to the bedroom. He stripped his shirt over his head. Tomorrow would be an exhilarating day of herding the ponies to the water, swimming them from Assateague to Chincoteague, then the parade to the fairgrounds. A full day on horseback would clear his head. Exhausted, Murphy crawled beneath the soft sheets on his huge bed. His mind emptied and he fell fast asleep.

CHAPTER SIXTEEN

The alarm blared and Murphy rolled to his side and slapped his palm on top of the screaming box. The red numbers flashed 4:00 A.M.

"Mercy," Murphy swung his feet over the side of the bed and grimaced. Kayaking had definitely hit a few of his lesser used muscle groups. Thankful there wasn't anyone present to watch him wince, Murphy padded gingerly to the massive bathroom to pay homage to the over-the-top ceramic tiled shower stall. Multiple shower heads slanted from three walls each with various stream settings. He set the water pressure to pulse, adjusted the temperature a fraction below scald, and groaned in pleasure as he stepped in. With a few adjustments, Murphy aimed the torrent of water allowing the blistering stream to massage his tight shoulders. The steam encased him and the wonder of hydrotherapy soothed his muscles, and chased the fog from his brain.

Murphy pulled on his faded jeans, well-worn boots and the event t-shirt Rudy had given him. He'd moved herds of livestock countless times but never through saltwater. The Saltwater Cowboys would swim the entire herd of ponies across the channel and into the fairgrounds. Chincoteague would be polluted with thousands of people hoping to create a life lasting memory at the sight of the wilds in the water. Murphy plopped his wide brimmed hat atop his head and grinned. Today was going to be a rush.

Murphy had met Rudy, driven across the bridge to Assateague and helped to saddle the horses, all before the sun had broken the horizon.

Saltwater Cowboys and volunteers milled about the acre of grassland preparing for the first leg on the drive. Boys and girls of all ages bustled with the vigor of youth offering donuts and drinks to fortify the riders for their journey. The organized confusion added a hum of life to the air. Beneath it all, the wild ponies whinnied softly in anticipation. Their calls laced together seamlessly like the strains from the finest orchestra.

Murphy tethered Buzz to the corral and sank his teeth into a soft powder dusted ball of dough. Rudy ambled toward him with two tall mugs of steaming coffee, "You ready for this Cowboy?"

"Thanks," Murphy accepted the mug, "I'm looking forward to it."

"We'll have some Sunday drivers who join in," Rudy sipped, then snarled, "Hot, hot, damn it that's hot." He pressed his hand to his lips. "Sorry, where was I? Oh yes, Sunday drivers…old timers and some retirees that just enjoy the pageantry. They'll hang to the sides; we'll do the muscle work." Rudy swept his hat from his head and rested his elbow on the fence post.

Murphy nodded, "So where do you want me?"

"You'll start up front with Sean and Boots, and then drop back as we move the herd into the marsh."

"Sounds good."

"Once we got'em into the wetland, we'll herd them along the shoreline until the slack tide can be calculated." Rudy stroked Buzz's nose. The big horse nuzzled Rudy's bald head gently. "Then, it's time for your favorite part, right buddy?" Rudy spoke directly to the horse now. "We'll jump those wild buggers into the open water and swim the channel." Rudy untied Buzz and handed the long reins to Murphy. "It's better than …" Rudy plopped his hat on top of his head and wiggled his brows suggestively. "Well use your imagination."

Murphy snorted out a laugh and led Buzz away from the rail.

It was nearing mid-morning when the cowboys urged the ponies from the corral to the paved beach access road. Usually crowded with morning bikers, joggers, and early beach goers, today the road had been blocked to ensure a quiet transfer for the ponies. Tails whipping at persistent flies, they tossed their manes and flicked their ears warding off the pests. To Murphy's amazement, the ponies moved together with a united sense of calm. No rush, as if they were herded everyday, the group moseyed along easily behind the lead horses.

As the group rounded the first bend, the serene drive hit its first snag, a gridlock of bodies. Tourists on bikes and lawn chairs swarmed the macadam road. Some were even perched on car roofs wheedling cameras and camcorders, as they cheered the ponies on.

"Madness," Murphy muttered.

"Tip of the iceberg, my friend," Rudy commented as they closed the last twenty-five yards to the gate. "Don't let the ponies' indifference fool you, Cowboy. When we push them into the marsh, they'll scatter like headless chickens." Rudy adjusted himself in the saddle. "Give Buzz a loose rein and he'll run with 'em."

Murphy nodded.

"Watch out for strays," Rudy continued, "especially the wee ones. They'll spook easy when they lose sight of their mommas. Peel off in pairs to pull 'em back. Standard stuff for you I'd imagine, right Cowboy? Let Sean and Boots take the lead and once they settle in and dawdle toward the shoreline, you work your way back to me."

"Sounds good."

The ponies took off like a shot just as Rudy had predicted. The throng of onlookers cheered and whistled, urging the ponies on. Buzz needed little encouragement from Murphy to follow the herd. His hooves churned the soft earth, as he surged forward attacking the marsh at a full gallop. It was nothing short of spectacular, Murphy thought, as he molded to Buzz's back and enjoyed the ride.

The dominant stallion shot across the vivid green marsh grassland. He pranced and threw his head in dissent at the mounted horsemen. Murky water splashed violently coating the underbellies of the horses and ponies. Murphy, Sean, and Boots pushed the pace and remained in front. In the distance Murphy heard Rudy shout out the order for the gate to be secured behind them. As Rudy predicted, a small group broke off. Murphy glanced over his shoulder and watched as Nub and Bobby deftly handled the strays.

The lead stallion slowed and settled into an easy trot. "Not too bad for firefighters," Murphy muttered just as a flash of color caught his eye. Instinct kicked, he pulled the leather reins firmly to the outside and squeezed his legs. Buzz leapt immediately to the answer the call of his rider and the two of them moved as one chasing down the rebel foal. The blur of color was none other than the little paint Murphy had brought in the first day. Spunk and spirit, the paint circled the marsh at an unyielding pace. The delighted onlookers cheered his mutiny. The relentless pursuit of freedom ended as the paint returned to the main gate to find it sealed and locked. Wildly the little colt twisted his neck and found Buzz and Murphy had cornered him. Wrangler mode took over and Buzz and Murphy put on an extraordinary show cutting off the paint's escape repeatedly. Finally Murphy unhooked his lasso and skillfully threaded it through his leather gloves. The loop whistled through the humid morning air, spinning above Murphy's head. The crowd sucked in a collective anxious breath as the rope shot out like a striking snake toward the dodging paint. Murphy's pinpoint accuracy had the lasso's loop sliding over the foal's neck. With a quick tug, the rope cinched taut, thwarting the foal's escape.

Communal 'Awes' of disappointment from the bystanders were quickly replaced by a rousing round of applause for Murphy's proficiency. Resigned to capture, the paint pranced alongside Buzz and together they trotted into the marsh.

When the foal had bolted, Rudy held back to watch the show and damned if it hadn't been worth it. Murphy's cocky grin was as bright as the morning sun as he pulled beside Rudy on Onyx. "Showin' off, Cowboy?"

"Not possible," Murphy beamed even more brilliantly. "Good is just good."

Rudy's laugh bellowed, startling the foal. The men picked up the pace and transferred the foal across the marsh without any further incidents.

The herd gazed freely along the channel. Saltwater Cowboys rotated shifts policing the group. Across the water, the excitement of the crowd could be seen, felt, but blessedly, not yet be heard.

"Look at all those people," Murphy said warily.

"Witnessing a slice of history today," Rudy said.

"But it's a lot of people..."

Sean laughed at Murphy, "You even have that many people back home in quiet Montana?"

"Probably, but they would never consider gathering in one place, at the same time." He shuddered "It's a wonder the island doesn't sink."

Rudy slapped him on the shoulder. "How about we talk about the swim leg of our trip and keep your mind off Chincoteague becoming the next Atlantis."

Murphy straightened and deliberately turned his back on the water. "So Rudy, what's the deal with slack tide?"

"Slack tide is the time when the tide is changing. High tide, the water moves in fills the bay, low pulls it out again. Between the two tides, there's a point where the water nearly stops moving."

"Very still water puts little strain on the ponies." Sean added.

"Makes sense," Murphy shifted again to observe the water.

"Not an exact science, it's Mother Nature you realize." Rudy snapped off a blade of beach grass and chewed on the end.

Sean mimicked the gesture, "That's why the advertisers say the swim will happen between 7:00 AM and 2:00 PM."

"We wait her out, Ms. Nature. If we'd guess, she'd switch it up anyhow, just to prove she could." Rudy tossed the grass into the water and hooked his thumbs in his jeans. "Women," he scoffed.

"Women," Sean echoed and made Murphy chuckle.

CHAPTER SEVENTEEN

The ponies rushed the water fiercely. Even the timid foals seemed to prefer braving the water to standing on the shore without their mothers. Nostrils flaring, the herd grunted and splashed as their strong legs churned the salty water and sandy channel bottom into a murky mix.

When the last pony was committed to the swim, Murphy eased Buzz into the water. Buzz was alert to Murphy's commands, but set his eyes on the ponies in front of him. Murphy kept his focus on the ponies too, making certain the foals didn't struggle in the agitated water. Across the channel, thousands of spectators cheered the swimming herd. Murphy marveled at the size of the crowd. People had even taken to the water to view the annual swim. Pontoon boats, jet skis, kayaks... there were people everywhere. Patrol boats lined the channel in an effort to keep the swimming lane open for the ponies.

It was insanity, and a primary reason Murphy favored the west. Crowds, sizable, screaming crowds made him twitch.

"Cowboy!" Rudy shouted, "Watch the flank. They'll get a bit squirrelly when they reach shore."

Murphy guided Buzz to swim in a circle allowing the herd to exit the water without pressure. What a picture they made, Murphy thought, as the strongest swimmers emerged from the channel. Their rippled muscled bodies, and tangled dripping manes, only added to the stunning vision the wild ponies made as they strutted boldly onshore.

Murphy spotted a commotion around the first foal climbing from the water. "First onshore," the loudspeaker barked, "This year first onshore is a...King!" The announcer squawked with excitement. "King Neptune is a seven month old tan and white. King Neptune will be given away by raffle drawing tonight at 8:00. Get your tickets and take home the King!"

The crowd cheered as the Saltwater Cowboys moved the herd into a waiting corral for recovery. The volume generated by the crowd roared in Murphy's ears.

"Loud ain't it, Cowboy?" Rudy grinned.

"Loud? I've heard loud, and this isn't it." Murphy scanned the mass of people. "How many are here?"

"It grows every year, probably 40,000 give or take."

"40,000...Good Lord," Murphy shook his head.

"Things'll settle in a few minutes. Bring Buzz over to the corral for a rest. Here comes Bobby, follow him."

The crowd was excited but controlled. They hadn't swarmed like Murphy had expected. After taking photos and getting a good look at the herd, spectators moved from the park to the streets to wait for the pony parade.

"Hey Murphy, nice mob don't you think?" Bobby snickered at Murphy's sneer. "What's the matter Murphy, don't like people?"

"I like them fine...in theory."

"Bread and butter, man." Bobby turned his mount in a tight circle then pulled next to Buzz. "Seriously, do the math, if even half of those people by an ice cream cone for two bucks...Cha-ching." He rubbed his fingers together. "They'll spend a lot more than that, but they'll leave having witnessed a piece of history in action."

Murphy nodded, "I get that, but…" He shuddered, "Too many for me. How 'bout you show me where Buzz and I escape for a bit and rest up before the parade."

Murphy followed Bobby to a corral where the horses were tethered. Riley, with a sack of red apples hugged tight to his chest, busily moved from one Cowboy to the next as he offered a treat for horse and rider.

"Hey Riley, you working hard?" Murphy threaded Buzz's reins through the wooden rail.

"Yeah," Riley's head hung a bit. "I didn't get picked to shovel poop in the parade."

Murphy stifled the chuckle. "You're upset 'cause you can't scoop poop?"

"Too many volunteers," Riley sulked. "So I have to hand out apples." He kicked the sand.

"Oh I don't know, I think Buzz is pretty stoked that you brought him a treat."

On cue, Buzz nudged Riley's small shoulder seeking the fragrant fruit. Riley shrugged and dug an apple from his sack and handed to Murphy.

"You give it to him."

The smile lit Riley's eyes, even though it barely touched his lips. "Rudy said I can scoop the poop on the return trip, but it's not the same. The people won't line the street like today."

That suited Murphy just fine. He scanned the thinning crowd. Moving toward the corral wearing a bright pink *Penning Event Staff* t-shirt, was Jess. Easy to pick out in neon pink, she had two cameras draped around her neck and a digital held out in front of her. Murphy watched her as she pivoted, constantly snapping candid shots of the action.

"Come here, Sport." Murphy hoisted Riley to the top rail and handed him an apple. Following Murphy's lead, Riley clenched the apple between his teeth. Jess aimed her lens at the pair of them with apples jutting from their smiles. She captured the image just as the horses on either side lifted their heads to nibble on the exposed sides of the apples, coaxing giggles from both Murphy and Riley. Rapidly shooting, Jess recorded the sequence like a motion picture until all of them were shaking with laughter.

Murphy settled Riley back on the ground as his boyhood giggles rippled. "Those will be great shots," Jess said. "Hey there, Cowboy."

"Jess," Murphy tipped his hat. "Photo duty?"

"Just for fun," she shrugged. "You're never certain 'til they are printed, but I think I have some keepers. Riley, I have the scooter if you want a lift to the fairgrounds."

"No, I'm gonna' walk in the parade, Momma. Got to make sure the guys don't miss any poop."

"A poop foreman," Murphy laughed.

"If you're sure. Please go get a sandwich before the parade. There's a tent by the water with food and drink for the staff."

"Sure Momma," Riley said as he raced off.

"Any moment he's going to drop," Jess shook her head. "He doesn't have a clue how tired he is."

"Adrenaline and youth," Murphy watched as Riley was swallowed by the crowd.

Rudy ambled over, "Hey Jessie girl." He draped his arm loosely over her shoulder. "Where's that boy off to?"

"Hey there yourself," Jess smiled up at him. "Riley's after food, what else? You and Murphy need to fuel up too. You've got a long day yet."

Rudy rubbed his belly, "I could eat."

"Keep an eye on my little man, would you? I've got to get over to the fairgrounds and help Kate set up." Jess eased away, "Have a good ride." She glanced over at Murphy, "See you later?"

"Yep, I'll be around."

Rudy figured he was as good as invisible when these two were locking eyes. "What 'ya servin'?"

"The usual," Jess backed away playfully. "Fresh peach ice cream and hot homemade pies..."

"Tease," Rudy muttered after her. "Herding drums up an appetite, don't it Murphy? Let's get us some fuel."

* * * *

The ponies seemed oblivious to the noisy horde of spectators lining the street. Fussing children, energetic teens, animated adults, and vibrant grandparents, you name it, the demographic was represented. Murphy and Rudy trailed behind the herd. From this vantage, Murphy could see Riley pointing out pony poop before it even contacted pavement.

"That boy's starting to wear down," Rudy commented. "Jess said he was bouncing on her bed before 4:00 AM. Said he pestered her until she finally dropped him at the corral just before 5:00."

Murphy noted Riley's sneakers were skimming the pavement. "You think Jess would mind if I gave him a lift?"

Rudy considered a moment and then smiled, "I think that she'd be alright with that." He hooked his thumb and index finger in his lip and ripped a quick ear-piecing whistle. Riley turned immediately and jogged toward Rudy and Murphy. "Call him like a dog," Rudy chuckled. "Hey boy, you tired?"

"I'm no weenie." Riley scoffed and thrust his fists to his hips.

"Too bad for you, I guess," Rudy clucked his tongue.

"Too bad, why?"

"Ask the Cowboy." Rudy urged Onyx to quicken his pace.

Riley shielded his eyes and tipped his face up to Murphy. "Well? Too bad why?"

"You want a lift?" Murphy asked.

"You mean it?" Riley's eyes lit excitedly.

"Unless you want to spot poop for your cronies for another half mile."

"I've seen enough poop. What's a crony?"

Murphy laughed. "A buddy, a pal."

"I get it."

Riley reached and clasped Murphy's arm firmly. With one powerful pull, Riley was lifted and settled across Murphy's lap. "Take the reins, Buddy." Riley held the saddle horn with his left hand and draped the leather loosely in his right. "Good, you're a natural. Buzz wants to follow the group so just keep him steady. I'm going to take a little nap."

"Cool..." he whispered with wonder. "Thanks Murphy."

* * * *

Jess heard the crowd cheering and knew the ponies must be in sight. "Mind if I go watch?" she asked Kate.

"Not at all. We're in good shape here."

Jess stashed her apron, grabbed her camera, and raced from the stand. Her bright event staff t-shirt helped to clear her path as she edged through the clusters of people. Standing in the center of the street, she captured the procession as it moved toward her. After a dozen shots, Jess moved quickly to the penning corral where the ponies would spend their time during the next days at the fairgrounds. She had learned over the years that if she stood on the auction platform, she could get great photos with limited spectators.

The ponies were led in by Bobby and Sean. Jess snapped a great shot of them looking focused and masculine in their saddles. The grounds crew swung the corral gates wide open. Troughs of cool water and a fresh blanket of straw beckoned the ponies inside. The large holding pen filled quickly. The cowboy escort peeled off and moved off to the stable to retire their horses.

Finally the gates closed and the remaining Saltwater Cowboys funneled into the grounds. Rudy and Nub were the next pair who walked into the fair grounds. Jess zoomed in on Rudy's face. Cheek loaded with tobacco, he winked and tipped his hat at someone in the crowd. Jess felt a smile tug at her lips. Good grace, the man was a charmer. She focused on the next horse and rider and was surprised when Riley's face filled her viewfinder. She clicked the shutter, automatically adjusting the lens to capture Riley seated confidently astride Buzz. Murphy's body framed Riley's as they moved toward the corral. Jess watched as Murphy leaned down and whispered something into Riley's ear. Riley nodded and a look of intense concentration veiled his tiny face. Murphy lifted his weight, slid off the saddle, and over the rump of Buzz. When his boots hit the ground, he grinned up at Riley and Jess read his lips when he said, "You got it kiddo, take him in."

Jess's palms were sweating. The rest of the fairground action was forgotten. She held the three of them, man, horse, and boy, framed within her view finder until they were no longer visible.

Slowly Jess lowered the camera and settled her hand across her belly. Her heart circled slowly inside her chest and then plummeted like a free falling skydiver until it twittered beneath her palm. "So that's what it feels like," she whispered to herself. "Jess, you're in deep trouble." She secured her camera and climbed from the platform. She needed to catch her head up to her heart...fast.

* * * *

Buzz was as tired as a horse that'd begun the day before sunrise could be. Murphy leaned over the stall's half door and stroked his neck. Rudy slid the latch on the neighboring stall securing Onyx. "Good day, huh Cowboy?"

"One of my best so far," Murphy leaned heavily against the door and removed his hat. "I'm no pansy when it comes to long hard days, so it's either the salt air or the night life around here that are weakening me." He scrubbed his hand across his face. "Damn, I'm tired."

Rudy stifled a yawn. "I won't tell if you don't. What would you say to a piece of fresh baked pie and a nap?"

"Amen."

"Ha!" Rudy clasped his hand on Murphy's shoulder. "Follow me, boy."

Jess had lost track of how many pieces of pie she'd passed across the counter. "The size of the crowd surprises me every year," Jess said to Kate.

"Good for the island," Kate handed her two more slices. "New faces... new memories..." Kate's voice grew wistful and feathered off.

"What are you...?" Jess stopped her question when she spotted Rudy and Murphy. Vacationers and locals stepped aside as the men moved easily through the sea of people.

"Jessie girl," Rudy said, "We need pie. Big, man-sized, pieces of pie. And Katie," he barked, "coffee, tall, hot, and black."

"P-l-e-a-s-e," Jess pinned Rudy with her best stern mother face.

"*Please* Katie," Rudy said so sugary sweet Jess couldn't help but roll her eyes.

"Enjoying your day Murphy?" Jess asked casually.

"Very much, thanks. Get any more shots with that camera of yours?"

Her thoughts trailed back to Riley and Murphy sharing the saddle. "I think I got some good ones." Jess smiled. "What kind of pie do you want, peach, apple, shoo-fly?"

"Yep that'd be perfect," Rudy interrupted.

"Rudy," Kate clucked her tongue.

"Just savin' myself a trip back to the counter."

Kate's face was stern with disapproval.

"I want a slice of each and at sixty some years old, I'm pretty much done explaining my thought process."

Murphy snickered at the two of them. "I'll just have peach please, Jess."

"Kiss-up," Rudy elbowed him.

"No, I don't care much for apple and shoes and flies don't sound appealing."

Kate laughed as she carried two plates to the window. "Here you go men. Murphy, I gave you a small slice of shoo-fly because it's a lot like those soft shell crab sandwiches. Sounds awful until you sink your teeth in."

"God's honest," Rudy forked up a bite. "Mmm…"

"Take it to a table," Kate shook her head. "Here's your coffee. Murphy, kindly lead that man to a seat."

Jess and Kate leaned over the counter shamelessly appreciating their exit. Kate fanned herself and whistled softly, "Gotta' love worn denim, huh girl?"

Jess snorted, "Kate!"

"Ain't in the ground, am I?" Kate draped her arm across Jess's shoulder and lowered her voice. "What are you planning on doin' with that Cowboy?"

"More than I had originally thought," Jess answered quietly.

"Mmmm…" Kate hummed.

Jess waited to be chastised for her foolishness.

"About damn time you had your bell rung," Kate said a bit too loudly.

"Kate," Jess hissed as she twisted around to see if anyone had heard.

"I'm just saying," Kate whispered, "good for you. When?"

Jess laughed weakly, "Is tonight soon enough for you?"

Kate gripped Jess in a tight hug, "Be safe."

"Yes, Mommy." Jess giggled.

Riley bounded up to the counter. "Momma did you see me riding in with the herd? Buzz was awesome and Murphy let me do the whole thing so he could take a nap."

Jess ran her hand down his cheek. "Yes, I saw you." She hoped she'd captured the range of emotions that were still visible in Riley's face. "Where are you off to now?"

"I'd like to do some rides if that's okay. Then if you say yes, the rookie 'Saltwater Helpers' are having a sleepover at the firehouse, so we can all be here early tomorrow. Rudy, Sean, and Bobby are chaperoning."

"I don't know buddy, you were up awfully early. I think dinner at home and an early bed. I want you to sleep well. I'll get you here on time tomorrow."

"Oh Momma…"

"I was hoping you'd want to invite Murphy over to thank him for what he did today."

Riley's pout softened as he toed the dirt thinking it over. "That'd be cool I guess."

"I'll make a deal with you. You go and invite him, and if he says yes, we'll sneak out of here; and if you take a solid two hour nap, I'll run you to the firehouse as soon as dinner is over. Deal?"

"Deal! Thanks Momma. What time should I tell him?"

"Anytime after 5:30 would be good," she shouted at Riley's back as he raced away. Moments later, Riley skidded to a halt beside the table where Rudy and Murphy were inhaling pie.

"Yuk," Riley examined their plates, "cooked fruit."

"Don't know what you're missin' Kid." Rudy forked up another bite. "It's an essential food group." He shoveled the apple into his mouth, "Pie."

"**Pie** is not a food group." Riley held out his fingers, "Dairy, fruit, meat, and grain. Not pie." Riley turned his attention to Murphy. "Momma wants me to invite you to dinner anytime after 5:30 'cuz I have to take a nap," he rolled his eyes, "and I'm not even tired."

Murphy glanced across the table into Rudy's stoic gaze. "Dinner would be great, Riley." Murphy said. He turned to face the little boy, "And you know 5:30 gives me enough time to sneak in a quick nap myself."

"You nap?"

"When I get up at the crack of dawn I do."

"Hmm," Riley chewed his lower lip and mulled this interesting bit of information. "I guess I could lie down for a little while. Catch you later." Riley ran off.

Murphy drank the last of his coffee. Rudy's expression had softened but he still studied Murphy intently. "You need to say something, Rudy?"

"You're good with him… easy." Rudy leaned back and rubbed his belly. "Got room for another piece?"

"No way, I'm stuffed," Murphy eased from the bench and stretched. "Actually I wasn't kidding; I am ready for that nap."

"Let's pester Kate into cutting us some slices for the road. I like to rile her up."

"You are terrible." Murphy followed Rudy to the counter to watch the battle.

CHAPTER EIGHTEEN

Poncho greeted Murphy at the car. Tail wagging, stick dangling from his mouth, the pup sat patiently hoping for a pat on his head.

"Hey there, Poncho," Murphy obliged the fur-ball in a generous rubdown. "What'd you bring me, huh?" He picked up the ragged stick and chucked it across the lawn. Thrilled, Poncho yipped out a happy bark and zipped off in hot pursuit.

Murphy shut the car door and turned toward the small cottage. Backlit by the setting sun, the cottage appeared like an intricate oil painting captured by the finest hand. Touches of light, shadow, and color, were enhanced by the delicate sounds of the bay waves as they lapped against the shoreline. The breeze off the water rustled the tree leaves hypnotically and although it was not yet dark, the porch light was on in welcome.

Silhouetted in the window, Jess worked in the small kitchen. Even though Murphy knew his feet were firmly planted, he surprisingly felt unbalanced.

Not blind or stupid this time, but he'd fallen flat just the same. Murphy decided he'd deal with the consequences another time. Every moment he had spent on this tiny island, especially with Jess, had made him a better man. "Let's get inside Poncho. These mosquitoes are anxious to munch on some flesh and I'd rather it not be mine."

Jess heard the crunch of the tires as Murphy pulled across the shelled drive. She had prepared herself all afternoon for this moment. Poncho barked excitedly and she heard the car door close. Jess found herself gripping the sink for stability. A gentle tap on the screen door jerked her back to reality. Leap or stand still, Jess thought as she strolled across the kitchen tile, and stepped onto the enclosed porch. Every wall she had built fell away when she saw Murphy, flowers clamped in one hand, a bottle of wine, and a two liter bottle of Coke cradled in the other. She pushed open the door, "Welcome, come on in."

Jess stood before him in a simple sundress and bare feet. Her hair was still damp from her shower, and around her neck, the sea glass they had discovered the day before hung on a leather cord.

Murphy crossed the small porch and stepped over the threshold into the kitchen. A fragrance hung in the air that reminded him of summer. Flower, fruit, sea, spice, he couldn't put his finger on the delicate scent, but he knew he'd never forget it. In front of Murphy sat a weathered round wooden table with four mismatched chairs tucked around it. A tall tapered candle surrounded by a glass sconce was centered in-between two place settings, waiting to be lit. Two...two place settings.

Murphy looked over at Jess. She appeared much like she had when he'd first seen her strolling across the sand, confident, carefree, and beautiful. She leaned casually against the door jamb, with one hand on her hip, while the other fidgeted with the seam running the length of her dress. There went that tug again...right in the pit of his stomach. "Riley?" Murphy asked in a low voice.

"Rudy has him at the firehouse for a rookie's celebration..." Jess's eyes stayed boldly on his, "overnight."

Murphy froze as her words sank in...*overnight*. A smile crept slowly across his face, and although he itched to close the distance between them, he held back. There was one very serious issue they needed to clear up. "Integrity?"

Jess sighed as she walked to the kitchen counter. With her back to Murphy, she opened a tin canister and pulled out a piece of rawhide. "Integrity is something I believe in with my entire being. It's the single thing that no one can take from you." Jess turned and faced him. "I have the power to choose. The power to make my own decisions, right or wrong."

Murphy nodded, but couldn't speak. She was radiant, confident, and destroying him with every passing second. Jess crossed the room slowly and stepped onto the porch. She pushed open the screen door and tossed the rawhide into the grass. Poncho scampered after the treat and settled down in the cool grass to chew. Jess flicked off the porch light. "For the little time we have," she walked back to the kitchen and gently shut the door, "I'm choosing you." The click of the lock sounded like gunfire in the hushed woods. Jess pressed her back against the door and absorbed the sight of Murphy standing in her tiny kitchen. She was actually trembling. Her heart may shrivel when he left, but for tonight, it swelled inside her chest.

Murphy sat the wine and soda on the table, and then took a single step toward her. He could see her pulse hammering along the side of her throat. Not as confident as her casual pose suggested. He stepped closer and he simply held out the bouquet of flowers.

It was Jess's turn to smile. She accepted the flowers and buried her nose in the colorful blossoms. She had expected him to whip her from the room like the frenzied pages of a hot romance novel; flying clothes, passionate kisses. He was throwing her off; not that she had formed an entire game plan.

Murphy shifted closer. The tips of his boots stopped just short of her painted toes. He framed her face with his strong hands, and kissed her lightly. "We can just have dinner you know."

Jess huffed in frustration, "I sure have lost my touch." She started to turn away.

"Hey now," Murphy eased her around until she faced him once more. He traced his finger across her cheek, then down beneath her chin. With a hint of pressure, he lifted, gently urging her eyes to meet his. "You haven't lost anything," he murmured as he touched his lips to hers. But he had... and he knew it.

The next kiss moved them through the kitchen. They danced their way along the narrow hall and into a small bedroom where soft music played. A wedding ring quilt hung on the wall behind the four-poster bed. Candles winked on the antique dresser. Blue and green glass jars placed on the deep window sill appeared to glow as they caught the final rays of the setting sun. Murphy held Jess at arms length and committed every detail of the room, of the moment, of her, to memory. He was undone.

Shaking his head, Murphy closed his eyes. Jess thought for a second he'd changed his mind, but when his eyes flashed open, the intensity in them stole her breath. She reached up and eased the straps of her dress from her shoulders. The fabric whispered down the length of her body, and pooled at her feet.

"Jess," Murphy said with wonder as she stepped toward him. He had no right to take so selfishly. There was still time to stop.

"Oh no you don't, Cowboy," Jess said, reading his mind. She lifted her hands to his face, "I'm choosing, Murphy." She looked deeply into his eyes. "I choose you."

Her gaze never wavered from his as she rose to her toes and kissed him. A soft promise of a kiss that offered...everything. Murphy's hands wrapped the small of her back and he reeled her in. Their kisses grew urgent, they held nothing back as Murphy's boots, denim, and cotton hit the floor.

A romance novel after all, Jess thought. Urgency gentled. Kisses lingered, hands caressed and as if time was an infinite commodity, they savored.

* * * *

Murphy pulled the comforter over them as the soft music played. He settled Jess against his chest and buried his face into her soft hair.

The sheer curtains lifted in the breeze, causing the candles to flicker as the cool air filled the room. Jess sighed inwardly as she snuggled in. Here it comes, she thought. It might have been years and she might have been a little rusty, but Jess didn't need any help remembering this part. The awkward *after*. Why had she thought she could handle casual? Sex was never casual. She had only fooled herself. It was going to crush her when Murphy left. Dumb, dumb, dumb, she scolded herself. Even now, as his easy breathing moved along the base of her neck, it was killing her.

The wind tossed the curtain again. "It's going to storm," Jess said and started to shift from the bed.

"Not just yet sweetheart." Murphy's satisfied voice rumbled against her skin. He shifted, and hugged her more securely against him. His lips brushed below her ear.

Tears came from nowhere. They tracked slowly down her cheeks soaking into the soft pillow.

Murphy knew she wept, and although a woman's tears were Kryptonite, he held her close. He had no words to comfort her. He didn't know how to tell her that he felt the same way. Joy and sadness. If he extended his vacation, it would only make things harder for them both. Murphy cuddled her closer and shifted so he could see her face. "Jess... please," he wiped her quiet tears.

"I didn't mean to fall apart on you," she sniffed, "I just need a moment."

Murphy kissed her damp cheeks. "Please Jess, look at me." When she did, her green eyes, bright with emotion, locked on his. If there was any consolation in that moment, it was that they understood neither of them was in this alone. "I need more than a moment," Murphy said as he lowered his mouth to hers.

* * * *

When Jess woke, the bed was empty. She sat up and wrapped the comforter around her chest. Poncho raced into the room and hopped on the bed. Fast footsteps padded down the hall followed by Murphy's irritated whisper.. "Damn dog, get out there before you wake..." He pulled up short as he took in the sight of Jess sleep-rumpled and a little shocked to see him.

"Morning," she said as she tucked the blanket more securely around her. "This guy giving you trouble?"

"No trouble, I found his food. I hope it's alright that I fed him." Murphy watched as she just stared at him. He walked over and kneeled in front of her. "Jess, are you okay?"

Her head bobbed up and down, but she said, "Nope."

Murphy smiled, "I know just what you mean. Do we have time for breakfast before we pick up Riley?"

"Rudy will take him to the auction. We've got time, first bid's about noon."

"Why don't you grab a shower and I'll whip something up for us."

CHAPTER NINETEEN

The fairgrounds were alive with activity. The rain overnight had soaked the ground and each degree the sun added turned the air into a sauna of dense, humid air. Murphy dropped Jess at the raffle table where she and some other volunteers solicited the crowd to purchase tickets. Prizes ranged from bushels of crabs and chartered ocean fishing trips to a Harley Davidson motorcycle and an eighteen foot boat and trailer. Not bad for a five dollar chance, Murphy mused.

Multiple vendors offered food and crafts, as well as collectible memorabilia depicting scenes of the round-up. The aroma of sizzling food enticed the crowd as it drifted throughout the festive atmosphere. Most of the interest was centered on the corrals of ponies. The herd had been split into three corrals. Stallions and older ponies not up for auction were penned by the road for viewing. Nursing mares were in another, and auction ready and unweaned foals were corralled beside the stands and auctioneer platform. Murphy strolled to the pen that held the separated youngsters and listened as the whinnies rang out from their worried mothers.

"Good group," Rudy stepped beside Murphy, "Should bring a fine profit." Sean and Bobby joined them and they all leaned on the rail of the corral studying the foals. "Now girls," Rudy teased Sean and Bobby, "Don't go blubbering all over yourselves when the little ones get carted off to their new homes."

"Same goes, Old Man," Sean shot back.

"Got your eye on one?" Rudy asked Sean.

"Could be..." Sean lifted his shoulder casually, "Sure as hell not tellin' any of you."

The men laughed heartily. Sean would take great precautions to make sure no one ran the price up on him again. The men's jeers faded and Sean's mind emptied when he spotted Zoe crossing the fairgrounds. Just the sight of her knocked him flat.

"Bobby," Rudy said, "You running the pony holders right?"

"Got it covered Chief," Bobby nodded.

"No one under fifteen years old in that pen or in the corral, Bobby and I mean no one. I want two holders minimum on each foal. Three if the little one is a wiggler. "

"No problem," Bobby pushed away from the fence. "I better head over to make sure I got enough hands."

"Sean," Rudy said curtly. "Are you planning on doing anything useful today other than drool and trade smiles with Zoe?"

"Yeah...I just might kiss her." Sean grinned as he walked off.

Rudy's laugh burst out. "She's clerking today," Rudy inclined his head to where Zoe was climbing up into the bleachers. "If he distracts her, we'll lose hundreds." Rudy pointed and clucked his tongue. He and Murphy looked on as Sean turned three shades of red while talking to Zoe. "Kid's got no brains, but..." Rudy eyed Zoe's long legs, "gotta' say he's got taste."

Murphy raised his brows at Rudy.

"What, am I dead?" Rudy shoved some fresh tobacco into his cheek. "What are you going to get into today?"

"Watch I guess, if you are sure you don't need help."

"Could be we'll need some help after the sale, loading ponies for transport. Most of the buyers are serious and are equipped to move 'em out. Later on we'll need to settle in the fall pick ups and make sure they're secured for the night."

The colt in front of them tipped his head and called for his mother. "Hard day for the babes," Rudy said softly and cleared the sentiment from his throat. "Get yourself a seat and hang onto it. Crowd will only get worse as the day moves on."

Rudy had been dead-on. The crowd settled in, filling the bleachers and grassy area around the corral. Standing room only. Thankfully Murphy was tall enough to see over those in front of him. Currently Boots and Nub were holding a chocolate brown colt around the neck. The anxious pony reared up at the unfamiliar contact of the men's hands. The auctioneer's gavel slammed down and the pony was sold for a tidy price of $450.00. A dozen or so of the youngsters had already been shown and sold. Most ponies were bought by people in the crowd, but occasionally they went to a silent bidder held by the auctioneer on a card in his pocket. Murphy was amazed by the diverse group of people in attendance. From Amish farmers to the obviously wealthy, the bidding and buying seemed to appeal to all.

Murphy saw Sean moving toward him with Riley's hand gripped firmly in his. Sean had bid on two foals so far, but had dropped out before winning. Riley lagged behind and was wearing an impressive pout as they joined Murphy.

"What's with the sour face, Sport?" Murphy asked.

"Momma won't let me get a pony, so I'm hanging with Sean till he drops his wad." Riley said.

Sean shook his head, "Stubborn little squirt." He handed Murphy a bottle of cold water. "Hot as a mother... hot," he amended. "My filly's up next."

"You gonna' get this one?"

"I didn't let on, but this is **the** one. She's my favorite."

Bobby and Rocco entered the circle gripping the buckskin filly. The auctioneer announced she was two months old and would be a fall pick up. Murphy eyed Sean whose hands were buried deep in his pockets as the first excited offers were made for the pony. The bidding grew serious and as others dropped out; Sean raised a finger and gained the auctioneer's attention. "$475.00," the bid was called and Sean entered the fray.

The volley was rapid and three players exchanged the lead. A man on the top row of the bleachers stood so everyone could see him. Dressed for an evening out, the man's wealth was obvious. His eyes tracked to the other bidders as he gauged how high he felt they would go.

Sean's eyes never left the auctioneer; his intent was plain on his face. The other bidder dropped out leaving only Mr. Money and Sean.

"I can't see, I can't see." Riley bounced on his toes. Murphy lifted Riley in one motion and deposited him securely on his shoulders. The bid jumped higher and higher, 550, 700, 750…

The kid had guts, Murphy thought as he watched Sean. Mr. Money winced as Sean inclined his head again, raising the bid to $900.00. The crowd rustled with excitement. To Sean's credit, his steely expression didn't waver. Murphy watched as a little girl grabbed Mr. Money's hand, grinning with excitement. The man looked down into her smiling face and raised the bid once more.

The bid returned to Sean who tipped his head yet again.

"He's gonna' get her, he's gonna' get her!" Riley quivered excitedly on Murphy's shoulders.

"Hush now," Murphy patted Riley's thigh.

"One thousand dollars," the auctioneer called. The man in the bleachers didn't move. It was up to him, raise or bow out. The auctioneer repeated the amount and the little girl gripped her father's hand. Murphy watched as the man shifted his weight and studied Sean. Mr. Money's knees softened and he sat gently on the aluminum bleacher.

"Daddy!" the little girl squeaked and burst into tears. He simply wrapped his arm around her and shook his head.

The gavel fell and Sean's face split with an earnest grin. He looked over at Murphy and then up to Riley, "Got her." Riley let out a whoop and cheered loudly. Murphy lifted him down and shook Sean's hand. "Well done. You bid as well as you play poker."

"That was great!" Sean said, as Riley raced in circles around them.

Next up was the paint colt Murphy had admired.

"He's a beauty too," Sean said. "But I can't buy two this year."

Nub and Andy held the fiery little guy as he tried to break free. The announcer read off that he was a fall pick up as Rudy had predicted and the offers began. The bidding rose like a fast paced poker game. The auctioneer pulled a white card from his pocket. "I'm holding 900." Anxious to see what the colt brought, Sean and Riley stood with Murphy looking on. "One thousand," the auctioneer called and the volley went round again. "I'm holding," The auctioneer held up his little white card.

"Man, I wonder how high the private bidder will go," Sean said. "I hate bidding against the card. I like to see who I'm playing against."

Murphy smiled over at him. "Good you already bought your filly then, huh?"

"Momma!" Riley called a second before he leapt into her arms. "Sean got the buckskin, she's beautiful! Do you want to go see?"

Jess laughed, "In a minute. I want to watch this one. He's my favorite." The paint tossed his head and stood arrogantly, nostrils flaring.

"1400...1500...16,17, 1800..."

"Oh my," Jess breathed in amazement, "So much money."

"Good for the fire department, right?" Murphy said quietly.

She nodded as the auctioneer called out again. The bidders were a woman and the little white card. Round and round they went. Finally the woman dropped out and the gavel fell. Applause rang out. "Highest sale of the day, Paint colt, sold for $3200.00."

"Holy cow," Jess said.

"Momma, can we go see Sean's filly?" Riley bounced excitedly.

"Lead on."

Murphy watched them disappear into the sea of people. The heat of the day was enough to melt your bones. He drank the cold water Sean had supplied and decided to find some shade.

Reclined against the trunk of a shade tree, Murphy smiled. A barefooted girl with long blond braided pigtails twirled in the sunlight. Simple joys he thought, as her calico print dress fanned out again. Why couldn't everything be as simple as twirling in the sun?

Armed with two ice cream cones, Jess found Murphy lazing under the tree. "There you are." She kneeled beside him, handed him the dripping cone, "Eat fast, they're turning to soup!"

Murphy licked the dripping cone. "Fresh peach, wow, thanks."

"Mmm-mm," Jess hummed.

"Where'd you leave Riley?"

"With Sean, Riley's angling to name the little foal. He'll pester Sean until his ears bleed."

Murphy's laugh faded as he looked at Jess's smiling face. She was beautiful, but there was more and he was neck deep in it. The ice cream melted and started to roll over his hand.

"Murphy," Jess wiped his hand with a napkin, "You're worse than Riley." She giggled and balled up the napkin. Murphy sat perfectly still, studying her seriously. Her laugh dried up. Her insides quivered. Captive in his gaze, Jess felt as vulnerable as a school girl. Murphy's eyes held hers and the sounds of the carnival faded. It was only the two of them. No bustling crowd, no loud speaker barking out bids. Just them.

Ice cream forgotten, Jess felt the shift from nervousness to delight. Murphy's hand tracked over her wrist and up to her elbow. Mesmerized she felt herself being drawn toward him, lost in the moment...

"Momma!" Riley flopped to his knees like only a child could; his legs contorted beneath him in an awkward 'W'.

Jess jerked back and Murphy watched as the pink crept into her cheeks.

"Momma?" Riley repeated.

Jess shook her head clear, "Yes honey."

"I named her! I named her, wanna guess? Guess! Guess!"

"Ethel, Mandy, Sandy, Trixie?" Jess spouted off a string of names.

"Susie, LooLoo, Miffy, Sally," Murphy joined the fun.

Riley wrinkled his nose, "Not even close. I named her, Montana 'cause Murphy brought her in and it's his first year and all."

Jess blinked in surprise. Riley looked expectantly at Murphy, "What do you think?"

Absurdly touched, Murphy patted Riley's knee. "Never had a foal named for me before. Montana, I like it. Good solid name. I'm honored."

Riley frowned and pointed at Murphy's melted ice cream cone, "You are sure making a mess of that."

"Yep," Murphy chuckled, "that wasn't my plan. How about you go get one for yourself and grab some more napkins." He dug into his pocket and handed Riley two dollars.

Jess watched the exchange and felt her throat closing. It was her turn to stare at Murphy. This big, strong, gentle, compassionate cowboy had stolen her heart, and he was halfway to stealing Riley's as well. Riley was getting attached. Jess would have to deal with that too when the time came.

Murphy studied Jess's somber expression. "I need to ask you something."

"All right." His tone alerted her that this didn't concern pony names and dripping ice cream cones.

"I know we are just getting to know each other. Would you consider...just think about...I don't know how it's done..." Murphy fumbled and felt like a teenager asking her to go steady. "Shit, I feel like an idiot. Let me try again. Can we stay in touch? Maybe try to, I don't know... date?"

"Murphy, if this is about last night, the tears, I'm sorry. I don't need you to turn your life upside down for me."

"This is about taking a step." Murphy laid his hand on her leg and took a bolstering breath, "I don't want to end this Jess, I want..."

She stared cautiously at his strong face, her green eyes brimming with emotion. "It's only been a few days, Murphy," she shook her head.

Riley thankfully picked that exact moment to interrupt. He tossed the napkins into Murphy's lap, "Raspberry, yum."

Mischief winked in Murphy's eyes as he observed Riley's purple lips, "You, tiny man, are working on a good mess yourself."

"Yeah, but I'm little; I'm supposed to be a mess."

Jess laughed and tugged Riley into her lap. Taking the next step...she considered Murphy's words. "Would you like to come over later, Murphy? Riley and I were going to finish the movie fest we started on date night. Someone..." Jess tickled Riley, "fell asleep on me."

"My belly was too full," Riley justified.

"Do I get over-buttered popcorn?" Murphy asked Jess.

"I think we could arrange that."

CHAPTER TWENTY

Murphy sat on the couch with his long legs stretched across to the coffee table. Riley, in soft *X-Men* jammies, had snuggled against him when the zombies crawled out of the woods. He stayed there, tight against Murphy's side, his eyes hidden, for the last thirty minutes of the movie. Now the little boy's breathing was deep and heavy as the credits rolled slowly up the screen.

Across from them, Jess was curled up on the love seat with Poncho. She had watched when Riley moved into the comfort of Murphy's body. She had watched little else as the two of them reveled in zombie invasion. Murphy's hand absently stroked over Riley's head as her baby slept. She folded the soft throw. "I'll take him to his room." She moved in front of Murphy.

"He's played out. I'll take him, show me where." Murphy scooped up the sleeping child and followed Jess along the hallway. Jess flipped on a dim nightlight and turned the comforter down. Murphy laid Riley on top of the bed and stepped back as Jess tucked the blanket around him and whispered a kiss across his cheek.

She turned to Murphy and held out her hand. Their fingers linked and they walked back to the living room. Jess switched the television to a music channel and the room was filled with classic rock. "Can you stay a little longer?"

Murphy merely nodded and drew Jess against his chest. "I'd like to talk a bit if that's okay with you."

They sat with the music drifting around them and Poncho sleeping by the door. They talked about the day, the island, about her career. They talked about Murphy's ranch, his family and visions for the future. "My grandfather had this way about him; I don't know how to explain it. He would never tell you what to do outright, but you knew what he was telling you anyway. He and my grandmother were incredible. I wish you could have met them." He trailed off.

Jess didn't have that kind of support. Her family was more self-serving, with Jess as the anchor. When she had come home from her senior year of college pregnant with Riley, and no father, they all but said, 'then who will take care of us?' "That's when I decided in order to carve out a life for myself and Riley; I had to separate physically from them." Murphy could hear the loneliness in her voice. "I worry sometimes that I did the right thing. Riley still talks with them on holidays and my mom calls on his birthday usually, but…"

Murphy pulled her close. "You have done well for yourself and Riley is thriving here, Jess. Survival is never an easy choice. When my Mom pulled up stakes with me and Tory, she left her whole life behind. I realize now, in order to do that, you either have to be desperate or incredibly brave. I think you are incredibly brave Jess."

He understood her and that was as comforting as the strong arm banded around her. She looked at him and smiled, "We didn't make any ground rules for tonight Murphy. Do we need to?"

He lowered his mouth to hers and kissed her lightly. "I think we are past rules now, Jess. We'll have to make them up as we go along."

Jess shifted toward him, her heart bursting with unspoken words, undeclared promises, and silent pleas. She framed his face and memorized every feature. With her eyes on his, she poured herself into the kiss. Murphy tightened his arms around her and pulled her across his lap, loving the way she fit against him.

Jess gripped his T-shirt and pulled him closer. *I want everything with this man*, the words screamed in her head. She gentled her hold on the cotton and rested her head on his shoulder and sighed deeply. Murphy's hand slid slowly up and down her back. Why was life so complicated? Jess burrowed closer, "I'd ask you to stay... I want you to stay."

"Not tonight. Riley is a great kid who is only halfway twisted. I'd hate to be the one who pushed him over the edge to corrupt." Jess pinched him. "Hey!" Murphy rubbed his side.

"What are you doing tomorrow?" she asked him.

"Nothing firm, what do you have in mind?"

"Come by in the morning, whenever you are up and moving." Jess walked him the door. "Bring any shoes besides boots, Cowboy."

"Sneakers work?"

"They'll do perfectly." Jess buzzed his lips with a quick kiss.

Murphy caught her hips when she would have slid simply away. "No you don't," he whispered and kissed her. Drifting on an impossible tide of feelings, Murphy eased back, "Goodnight Jess."

"Night Murphy," she sighed as he strolled into the night.

CHAPTER TWENTY-ONE

Jess took the lead with Riley behind her and Murphy brought up the rear. It had been ages since Murphy had ridden a bicycle, let alone on a hard road with traffic. Jess said they weren't going far, and Riley had told him to stop whimpering... Actually what he'd said was, 'Jeez Murphy, don't be such a sis. It's not like there are any hills on the island'. Murphy was certain his coolness factor had slipped a few notches.

The trio peddled down the unlined road past Chincoteague High. The school had served as the transportation hub the day before, shuttling spectators to and from the penning activities. As Murphy peddled past the building, he could see the H*ome of the Ponies* score board in the end zone of the football field, sporting an enormous wooden cut-out of a rearing stallion. The image of the powerful pony overlooked a small work crew converting yesterday's parking lot back into a football field.

"Momma," Riley called, snapping Murphy's attention back to his ride. "It's not far now, can I go in front?"

Jess looked over her shoulder and saw no traffic coming from behind. "All right, but stop at the fence."

Riley's tiny legs were a blur as he zoomed past her.

"Careful," she said with a shake of her head. Murphy kept pace with Jess as they eased into a small paved lot. A split railed fence marked the edge between the lot and the dense forest. There was an opening wide enough to walk or push a bike through and a permanent sign which read: No motorized vehicles beyond this point.

"This is a one mile walk/bike path maintained by the nature center," Jess explained. "About five acres of forest and water holes. If we are lucky, we might see some deer, black squirrel, and of course, lots of species of birds." Jess eased her bike beside Riley, "you stay behind me and keep as quiet as you can."

"I know the drill," Riley scuffed his sneaker.

"Well Murphy's new, so show him how." Jess eased her bike carefully through the split in the fence and veered off to the left. Riley followed close behind, and soon Murphy too slipped through the fence. The path dipped slightly downhill so they were coasting. There was a body of water off to the side and a group of birds were bathing and resting. Jess abruptly put her feet down and Riley and Murphy stopped quickly.

"There," Jess pointed to a fallen tree. Hanging upside down was a black squirrel. Frozen mid-descent, the little creature eyed the pedaling group just as curiously as they examined him. Deciding there was no imminent danger, the squirrel leapt from the tree trunk and disappeared into the brush.

They mounted their bikes and started off again. Riley skirted around Jess, "I'll lead, Momma."

"Keep your head up and watch for walkers." Jess called after him. She spotted a form ahead on the path, "Walker! Riley, WALKER!"

"That's not a walker," Riley hollered back, "That's just Kate."

Sure enough, the figure moving into view was Kate in a red velour jogging suit. "Morning all," Kate said as she smiled at Jess and Murphy knowingly. "Perfect day for a ride huh, Sporto," she said to Riley. "I heard you got to name Sean's new filly."

"Montana," Riley said proudly. "We are riding over to see her after this. She's a fall pick up. Sean told me to make friends so she'll be used to me when they move her to the farm."

"Sounds like a good idea," Kate ruffled his hair. "Riley, can you be extra quiet?" His head bobbled. "By the bridge," Kate whispered, "two deer."

"Momma, can we go? They might still be there."

"Go on ahead, quietly."

Riley hitched his foot on the pedal, "Comin' Murphy?"

"You bet."

Kate and Jess watched them peddle around the bend. "Nice picture you all make," Kate remarked.

"Don't get fanciful on me," Jess shook her head.

"Me?" Kate batted her eyes innocently. "Not a fanciful bone in my body."

"Could be that's what's wrong with ya'," a gruff voice muttered behind them.

"Who in damnation…" Kate trailed off as Rudy chugged around the bend.

"Mornin' ladies."

"What are you doing out here?" Kate asked.

"Doc says walkin's good for my heart." That was only half the truth. Rudy had also known Kate walked this trail most mornings. "I'm heading to the fairgrounds in a bit…paperwork. Auction tally's lookin' good," Rudy said. "Got four private bidders driving in today to settle up, but mostly the hard work is finished."

"Murphy's up ahead with Riley," Jess said. "Kate saw some deer by the bridge.

Rudy's eyebrows raised, but there was something in Jess's tone that caused the smart remark he readied to lodge in his throat. "I think I'll wander that way."

"Troublesome man," Kate clucked her tongue. "He was about to meddle in your business."

"Unlike you, I suppose." Jess laughed.

"I'm not meddling, I'm encouraging. There's a huge difference."

"I'd better catch up if Riley wants to visit Montana. Enjoy your walk."

"Have a safe ride." Kate watched as Jess disappeared around the corner. "Youngsters..." she muttered and noticed Rudy heading back her way, "...and old birds," she scoffed. "You're moving in circles, old man."

"I changed directions is all," Rudy joined Kate. He had become accustomed to the flutter the sight of her brought to him. But lately it was more a thunder of hooves rather than a beating of wings.

"Got something to say?" Kate thrust her hands to her hips under his scrutiny.

"May I walk with you?" Rudy said softly.

Surprised, Kate cleared her throat. He always picked at her or wanted to argue, but today there was something behind his eyes. Something...tender. "Of course you can. I've been having a lucky morning, deer, black squirrel...who knows what my luck might bring me next." As Rudy fell in step beside her, Kate acted on impulse and slipped her hand through the crook of his arm.

"Your good fortune is rubbing off on me, Kate." Rudy laid his hand on hers. "Could be the luckiest day I've had in years." They moved slowly down the path and into the shadows of the morning forest.

Riley was tireless, Murphy thought, as he pushed the pedals faster. Jess was out in front like a pace car. Riley hugged her rear tire, itching to take the lead. Finally, Jess turned on the last long stretch of road which led to the fairgrounds. She slowed her bike and allowed Riley to pull beside her. "You stay on the edge of the road and go directly to the corral."

"Thanks Momma!" Riley took off like a shot. His tiny legs propelled the bike to warp speed.

Murphy peddled until he was parallel with Jess. "You and Riley do this a lot?"

"At least three or four times a week." Jess smiled, "Helps wear him out. How are you holding out? I'd bet your sweet bottom's felt better."

"Does it show?" Murphy grimaced, "Wouldn't want Riley to think I'm a pansy." Jess chuckled as Murphy added, "Bike seats sure aren't as friendly as a saddle, that's for sure."

Murphy followed Jess into the shaded grove. She leaned her bike against a tree next to Riley's. "We better lock 'em up. There are still a lot of people roaming around. I'd sure hate to have to walk home."

Jess and Murphy secured the bikes then strolled to the corrals. One pen secured the herd to be returned to Assateague in the morning; the other held the fall pickups and their mothers. Montana, the buckskin foal, stood beside her mother, nursing.

Riley was seated on the top rail of the fall pickup corral, watching Montana.

"Hey now," Jess scolded when she and Murphy joined Riley at the enclosure. "You know better." She lifted Riley down, "Two feet on the ground, little man."

Riley moaned and reached his hand through the fence. "I want to touch her."

"Not just yet," Murphy voice was gentle as he crouched next to Riley. "What Montana needs is to see you, hear you, and smell you."

"Smell me?" Riley wrinkled his nose.

"Yes, she needs to get big whiffs of that kid stink you got all over you." Murphy poked Riley's belly gently. "Once Montana gets used to seeing you and hearing your voice, she won't be afraid when her mother leaves."

"Hmm," Riley considered Murphy's advice. "So I need to let her look at me while I look at her?"

"It's how the best partnerships are started."

Riley shrugged, "That's cool."

Jess listened to their easy exchange.

"How many horses do you have on the ranch Murphy?"

"Forty or so, I guess. They aren't all mine, and my sister Tory rescues neglected or abused animals from time to time, so…"

"Wow," Riley said with wonder. "Any little ones?"

"Yep, I've got some foals due in the next few months."

"So they will need to smell your man stink too."

Murphy chuckled, "Yes they will."

"Can I come see them sometime?"

"Riley," Jess scolded. "You don't invite yourself."

"Yes," Murphy spoke over her. "You and your mom may come anytime and stay right on the ranch."

"Could we Momma?"

The light in Riley's face broke Jess's heart, "We'll see."

"That means no," Riley's head hung.

"No, that means, we-will-see," Jess said slowly.

Riley looked at Murphy, "If she had said 'Maybe' I'd have had a better shot."

Murphy laughed "Is that how it works?"

"Riley," Jess rolled her eyes, exasperated.

"He's just explaining how it works, Jess." Murphy stood and reached for her hand. "You both are welcome any time. Will you think about it?" He held her gaze.

Murphy's pleading eyes were nearly as bad as Riley's. "Maybe," Jess said before she thought better of it.

"Yeah!" Riley's excited outburst spooked the horses.

"Shh now," Murphy snickered, "I got you a maybe, kid."

CHAPTER TWENTY-TWO

The morning sky was dull and overcast. Riley had been right; the excitement was much lower for the ponies' return swim. Diehard locals had still lined the street, but when they arrived at the channel to await slack tide, the Saltwater Cowboys were practically alone with the ponies.

Riley, poop foreman for the return swim, stood with Rudy and looked across the water. Murphy watched the surly fire chief as he stood with the chattering boy at his hip. Riley mirrored Rudy's stance, hands rammed deep in the pockets of his jeans, booted feet braced wide; they looked like bookends. Rudy, attentive to Riley's torrent of unending questions, finally hooked him in a headlock and playfully rubbed his head. Murphy looked on as the gruff chief kissed the top of Riley's tousled head and sent him on his way.

Murphy led Buzz to the water's edge. "What's Riley wrangling for?"

"Got a read on him, don't ya'" Rudy loaded his cheek with tobacco. "First he wanted a detailed explanation of slack tide, which I realize now was butter to grease the wheels of what he really wanted."

"Which was?"

"The boy felt I owed him for makin' him wait to scoop poop, so he suggested I pay up by allowing him to ride across the water with the herd."

"Can't blame him for trying," Murphy's smile was wide with approval.

"Nope, I sure can't," Rudy laughed. "When I said 'maybe next year' and pulled out my chew, Riley told me if I kept loading my cheek with crap I might not be around to ride with him when he gets old enough."

Murphy's' brows shot up, "Ouch."

"Yeah, low blow even for a squirt. He even smoothed it all out when he told me he wouldn't rag on me if he didn't love me."

"Nicely done," Murphy commented with sincere admiration.

"He makes me so proud," Rudy grinned. "Let's mount up."

Buzz tossed his head in anticipation as Murphy swung into the saddle. Freedom within reach, the ponies danced restlessly, itching to begin their swim. Rudy shifted Onyx into position at the edge of the channel, gave the signal, and the Saltwater Cowboys moved the herd into the water.

Eyes wide, nostrils flaring, the ponies attacked the water. It was considerably easier to move the group without the foals. Seemingly within minutes, the herd climbed on the shore of Assateague. Bobby, Boots, and Gus galloped in front, thwarting their rush to freedom. The cowboys circled the ponies so they could rest and be evaluated once more.

Murphy noticed a couple of the mares were exceptionally drained. "Couple of those mares are pretty winded," Murphy said to Rudy when he joined him.

"Not unusual," Rudy answered. "They don't rest well on the fairgrounds, and they don't like having their babies stripped away. It's hard on the girls. We'll give 'em thirty minutes and then you'll need to show me your skills Cowboy, if you got any." Rudy dug his pouch of tobacco from his shirt pocket. "We'll need to cut the herd back into the groups we found them in and scatter them over the northern marsh."

"Sounds good," Murphy said.

Sean rode over to join them. "I'm going with you Murphy. We'll take the Northern herd."

"That's a troublesome group," Rudy shook his head, "Who else you takin'?"

"Nub and Bobby," Sean sat tall in his saddle. "We can handle it Chief."

Rudy shoved a fresh wad of tobacco in his cheek and eyed the youngster. "Go on then, get to it."

Cutting the herd was a blast. Murphy and Buzz showed off as if they'd been teamed together for years.

"Makin' me look bad," Rudy muttered and spat in the grass.

"Not bad," Boots grinned devilishly, "Old maybe, but not bad."

"I'll show you old, princess." Rudy spurred Onyx. "I'll finish, Cowboy," he called to Murphy. "Take your group to the North."

Murphy tipped his hat and gave a sharp whistle to Bobby and Nub and Sean to fall in. The ponies tossed their heads in protest as the men moved into position. The dominant stallion pranced mightily and then reared boldly, slicing the air with wild hooves. Murphy and Buzz faced the stallion and held their ground. With a final valiant effort to show dominance, the stallion whinnied loudly before he bolted into the meadow.

* * * *

Jess looked over the roped off section of sand. Above her an *Oystercatcher* screeched loudly in protest. "I'm helping buddy. I'll be out of here in a moment." After a quick tally of hatchlings and eggs still waiting to crack, Jess moved to her four-wheeler and recorded the data. She was always concerned on the day the ponies were returned to the wild. The vulnerable nests, even roped off, wouldn't deter the excited herd as they moved back to the open marsh. So far, none of the preserved nesting areas had been trampled, and she had just a few more to check on. Jess fired the engine and moved north.

Kneeling in the soft sandy berm, Jess gathered the broken shells of a *Plover's* nest. "Predators," she mumbled. The *Plovers* would group their nests together to help provide security, but raccoons and gulls and even foxes could find the eggs and enjoy a fine feast. They hadn't gotten them all and in Jess's mind, that in itself was a small victory. She recorded the information in her log and started to pack up.

Jess climbed on the ATV and was about to move on when she noticed a lone rider moving across the dune. She lifted her hand to shield her eyes. It only took a moment for her to recognize Rudy astride Onyx.

"Hey girly," Rudy shouted. "What you up to?"

"Checkin' nests, what about you?"

"Onyx and I are taking a stroll," Rudy smiled at Jess. He knew she worried over the hatchlings and had hoped he'd find her on the dunes. He needed to talk to her. "Could you spare an old man a bottle of that water I know you've got stowed in the cooler?"

"I don't see any old guys, but yeah, I can spare a bottle."

Rudy dismounted and dropped Onyx's reins in the hot sand. He joined Jess at the four-wheeler and together they sat side by side on the bumper. "Jessie girl, I need to apologize for meddling in your affairs."

"There's no need for you..."

"Hear me out," Rudy patted her knee and then drank deeply. The cool water rushed down his throat, giving him time to gather his thoughts. "Bachelorhood has soured me some to young love. It takes a certain kind of heart to give fully to another; just as it takes a certain kind of strength to accept the loss of love. Love can hurt as much as it fulfills," Rudy stared across the dunes. The tall reed leaned heavily against the ocean breeze. "I see you as my own daughter, Jessie, and I know in trying to protect you, I tend to get stupid. You've already had so many hardships..." Rudy lifted her hand gently in his. "I love you. You deserve...everything, Jessie girl. The best that life and love have to offer you."

Tears tracked across her cheeks. She leaned her head on his shoulder. "I love you too."

"Does Murphy fit you like I think he does? Does he balance something inside that makes no sense?"

"It could never work."

Rudy shook his head, "Not what I asked, does he fit you?"

Jess sniffed, then nodded miserably, "He does, but," she shrugged. "The timing is off."

"You listen to me," Rudy straightened and looked Jess straight in the eyes. "Grab your happiness. Don't be the fool I was and think living solo protects you from hurt. It just makes you lonely. At the end of the day, you need someone to share the minutes with; the highs and lows and the moments of nothing. Our existence is fragile; our hearts are easily broken. You have to love to feel joy and you have to love to feel hurt, but you got to love or your life don't mean squat. Sixty years gives you an appreciation for such things. Once in a lifetime means just that, Jessie, once. Grab it with both hands and hold tight." Weariness laced his words, "I've spent my entire life waiting on timing and I've ended up alone." Rudy's voice was nearly inaudible. "I watched her grieve; watched time pass by while I waited to get the courage and grab what a youthful boy thought was a fanciful dream." Rudy sighed and finished his water. He hadn't meant to shift the conversation to himself, but it was too late. "Grab your life Jessie.

Make your way, you always have. Murphy is a good man, you know."

Jess hugged him. "You know it's not too late for you either Rudy. Riley's spending the evening at Kate's. Scrabble night, fried chicken, and fresh peach pie. Go referee. I'll be by to pick him up about sundown, and then you can make your move."

Rudy scrubbed his hand under his chin. "You meddlin' Jessie girl? How about I drive this toy back to the Nature Center and you take Onyx for a ride up the beach."

"Now who's meddling?" Jess smiled, and kissed his cheek. "And it's a work vehicle. No donuts in the sand, and watch out for my nests."

"Spoil sport."

* * * *

The off road access section of the North beach was closed to allow safe passage for the ponies. Sean and Nub took front flanking and Bobby and Murphy held the rear. It was easier going since the foals were out of the mix. But still wild ponies were wild, and every so often, an independent pony would prefer to take a different course.

"How much farther, Sean?" Bobby called out.

"Two, three miles, Rudy wants this group close to the state line."

The ponies were tired but as the cowboys moved them over the dune, they found a burst of energy. Their marsh home was in sight. Sean and Nub peeled off and joined Murphy and Bobby. "One final push, men," Murphy said. The group rushed the herd from behind and sent the ponies to freedom. The cowboys stood with the horses shoulder to shoulder watching as the herd galloped away.

"Awesome sight, ain't it?" Nub said. "I got some water stashed at the temporary corral. Let's tether these horses and watch the ponies settle in."

It didn't take long for the ponies to realize they were no longer being supervised. The mares relaxed and started to graze. Insolently, the dominant stallion stood, head high, stance wide, as he faced down the wranglers. Boldly his eyes challenged the men, clearly stating these ponies were his. He tossed his head to the wranglers in the distance and finally strutted into the high grass.

Murphy, Sean, Nub, and Bobby were seated on the top rail of the corral. The ocean rolled in and out behind them, the breeze steady from the water to the dunes.

Sean turned from the herd and looked over the rolling ocean. "I just don't get tired of looking at it."

"Different every day," Bobby said.

"Call Hallmark already," Nub quipped.

Sean cracked up, "Slipping into Rudy's role there, aren't ya Nub?"

"Someone's got to keep you girls from polishing your nails."

"Speaking of girls..." Sean inclined his head to a galloping form coming up the beach. Moving across the sand was Onyx. His hooves pounded the frothy surf. The force projected sand and salt water up, splattering the jean clad legs of Jess.

Nub let out a long low whistle, "Hallmark could take that picture."

Murphy had to agree. Mounted comfortably on Onyx's back, Jess sat tall in the western saddle. Her long legs hugged Onyx as she eased him to a trot and turned him from the surf. She closed the remaining distance to the corral confidently. "Men," she said as she led Onyx to the enclosure.

"Jess," they answered in unison.

"Workin' or done?" she asked.

"Enjoying the view," Sean said and realized he was staring at Jess. His face filled with color, "Oh, I mean..." Sean stuttered, "Scenery. We...um, were...a"

"Don't swallow your tongue, boy," Nub laughed. "We're headed in, Jess. What are you up to?"

"I was hoping to steal Murphy."

Murphy smiled at her.

Nub slid from the rail, tossed Jess a sly wink, and rapped his fist lightly on Sean and Bobby's thighs. "Girls, Let's saddle up."

Bobby's leather boots hit the sand. He nudged Murphy's leg as he passed, "You sure dumped us quick."

"That's 'cause the man's no fool." Nub pinched Sean's shoulder. "Come along boy."

"Good-bye guys," Jess laughed at the exiting trio. Cockily she tipped her head and grinned at Murphy, "How about a ride?"

"Yeah, let's do that."

They galloped the horses along the surf to the northern most point of Assateague. The state line was marked by a border fence that separated Maryland and Virginia. "Keeps our ponies where they belong," Jess explained.

"Does Maryland have ponies?"

"Yeah, but I'm not sure how they manage their herd. Different state, different rules. Want to turn back?"

"Not just yet."

"Want to swim?"

Murphy raised a questioning brow, "Swim?"

"Yeah, I think Buzz and Onyx want a swim."

Murphy glanced down at his jeans, which finally had dried from the channel swim earlier.

Jess swung her leg over Onyx and dropped to the ground. "I'm swimming, how about you big guy?" She nuzzled Onyx's big black neck. "Want to swim with me?" He tossed his head and whinnied as if agreeing with her. Jess released the girth strap and the saddle and blanket slipped from Onyx's back. She walked to the fence and propped the saddle and blanket out of the sand. Jess eyed Murphy as she shimmied out of her jeans. "Well Cowboy?" She stripped her t-shirt over her head and revealed her bathing suit.

"Planned this, I see." Murphy slid from the saddle and handed the reins to Jess. "I don't have a suit, you realize." He removed Buzz's gear and propped it on the fence as Jess had done. He kicked off his boots and walked toward Jess. "Boxers break any laws?"

"No one here but you, me, and the horses," she grinned at him. "I certainly don't plan to turn you in."

Murphy's hand paused on the button of his jeans, "Enjoying the show?"

"I'm not dumb."

Murphy tossed his jeans aside and laughed at himself. "This is a first."

Jess examined Murphy's Penning event t-shirt and black boxers. She tipped her head to the side, "Lose the shirt, Cowboy." In a swift move, Murphy stripped the cotton up and over his head, revealing that rock-solid torso that made her mouth water. Jess swallowed hard and passed him the reins. "Give me a leg up?" He laced his fingers together and hoisted Jess aboard Onyx's bare back. Murphy grabbed a handful of Buzz's mane and easily vaulted on. "Let's go." Jess said, and led Onyx into the salty water.

The horses didn't hesitate. They moved easily through the surf as the white water rolled toward them. To Murphy's surprise, instead of shying away as the waves bore down, the horses jumped. The rise of the rushing water cradled their massive bodies while below the surface, their powerful legs cut through the water. It was exhilarating and nothing like the swim during slack tide. The water pushed and pulled at Buzz and Murphy simply held a loose rein and enjoyed the ride. He'd never experienced anything like it. Buzz followed Onyx twenty yards from shore, then playfully swam in circles around one another.

Jess tipped her head back and stretched out her arms. "Isn't this the greatest?"

Murphy decided great didn't begin to cover it. She was breathtaking. He wished he could capture the vision of her surrounded by the summer ocean, bathed in the mid-afternoon sun, astride a swimming horse. Magnificent.

"Grab his mane and let your body float on the surface." Jess demonstrated. Murphy followed her lead, careful to keep his body away from Buzz's churning legs. He felt like a superhero.

Laughing, Jess pulled herself upright as the horses turned for the beach. Her face was lit by the reflecting sun. Water droplets sparkled from her shoulders as she looked over at Murphy. Her green eyes knowingly stated the power of the moment they were sharing. The horses handled the surf easily and moved regally on shore. Jess rode Onyx to the fence row and dismounted. She tied the bridle reins to the saddle horn and stroked Onyx's massive neck. Murphy jumped into the hot sand and secured Buzz as Jess had.

Jess unhooked her tote from the leather saddle, slung it over her shoulder, and held her hand out to Murphy. "Let's go dry off."

Together they moved across the vacant beach away from the animals. Jess opened the tote, pulled out a woven blanket, and stretched it across the sand. She dug into her bag again, and tossed Murphy a bottle of water and an apple. "Not much," she shrugged.

Murphy sat on the blanket, "I wish it was sunset."

"You'd be eaten alive by mosquitoes if it was sunset," Jess chuckled.

"True, but if it was sunset and this was a private beach, we could..." he reached for her.

"Yeah... that would be..." Jess allowed herself to be drawn to the blanket and into his arms. Murphy kissed her with a gentleness that had her heart swelling in her chest. He rolled her beneath him and lifted enough to push her wet hair from her face. "What's wrong Murphy? Don't want to end this day with an arrest for lewd conduct in public?" Jess teased and nipped his chin.

"Not particularly." He closed his eyes as Jess kissed his jaw, his cheek, and then sunk back into his willing mouth.

"How do you feel about anticipation?" Jess asked with that flirty sass he'd come to adore.

"I guess it would depend..." Murphy rolled quickly pulling her across his chest, "on what I'm anticipating." He captured her lips again.

Jess pushed up and her hair fell down like a curtain around them. "Riley is over at Kate's until nine," she whispered.

"Forget about drying off." Murphy smacked a swift kiss to her smiling mouth, lifted her body, and playfully set her aside. "Let's get going."

Jess pressed her hand firmly to his chest. "Anticipation, Murphy." She slid up and over his long body. "I'll make it worth your while."

Murphy gripped her waist and anchored her tight to him, as the blood abandoned his brain. He had to work to remind himself that they were on the open beach. "Jess..."

The warning in his voice only fueled her excitement. Her hands roamed over his chest, shoulders, and strong arms. Murphy linked his fingers through hers to stop their busy exploration, and groaned. Unable to take her assault any longer, he flipped them, reversing their position. The switch happened so quickly, Jess lost her breath. Murphy decided turn-about was fair play and began his own brand of torture. He traced her lips with his tongue. "No you don't," he scolded when she tried to rise up and capture his mouth. "Anticipation....this was your idea."

"I've changed my opinion," she laughed tightly. "Incarceration sounds better."

Murphy leaned on his elbows and studied her flushed cheeks and wet lips. His deep blue eyes roamed over the features of her face.

Jess felt treasured. The smell of the ocean, the cloudless sky, and the warmth of the sun... This was a moment in time she'd never forget. Her heart thundered with words she couldn't say. She twined her arms around his neck and drew him down. "Murphy," she said on a whisper of breath and poured every ounce of her feelings into the next kiss.

CHAPTER TWENTY-THREE

The north beach was deserted. It felt as if they were the only people on the entire island. Onyx and Buzz ambled along the firm wet sand. "Another perfect day," Jess said.

"Day's not over yet," Murphy winked at her. "What time do you need to get Riley?"

"I told Kate I'd be over before nine. She told me to call first in case Riley wrangles a sleep over."

"Kid's lucky, if you ask me; having so many people in his life that care about him."

"Yep, we fell into a good spot here."

The silence spun out. "Jess, I want you to know that I meant what I said to Riley about you coming to the ranch... You are both welcome anytime."

"That would be a big trip..."

Murphy eased Buzz to a stop and Onyx instinctively stopped also. "I want you to understand it wasn't a casual offer. In fact I have never asked another woman to make the trip. Consider it."

"We'll see," Jess said quietly.

Murphy's smile didn't reach his eyes. According to Riley's code, 'we'll see' meant 'not a chance'.

The horses entered the wildlife circle. Murphy knew he had to up his game. He needed to figure out how to convince Jess that what they were sharing could be a beginning. They could do the long distance thing until she felt more secure about moving to the next level. Lots of variables to consider, some were as simple as geography. Others, like the workings of a woman's mind, were out of his league. Murphy knew the only female to help him out was his sister. He needed to talk to his big sister, the sooner the better.

"Hey Jess, after we take care of the horses, how about some dinner?"

"I need to run into the Nature Center, then go home and check on Poncho, but dinner sounds great. You want me to meet you at the Inn? They have live music tonight."

"How about something quieter? What do you say to early dinner at my place about five?"

Jess couldn't think of anything better. "Perfect, what can I bring?"

"Your appetite, your dancin' shoes, and since your integrity has made room for me, that should be enough."

"You're on, Cowboy."

Chapter Twenty-Four

Murphy tossed his keys on the counter and glanced at the kitchen clock. It was just after four o'clock. He needed to work some fast magic. He slipped the grocery bags on the island and dialed Tory.

"Okay, I've got boneless chicken, shrimp, spinach fettuccini, fresh parmesan, olive oil, and salad stuff. Where do I start?"

"How much time do we have?"

"An hour."

"Good Lord Murphy," Tory clucked her tongue. "Clean the shrimp, put the chicken in the EVOO, add garlic, salt, and pepper. Then fill the pot with salted water for the pasta, and find the cheese grater."

"Evoo? What's an evoo?

"Murphy," Tory huffed, "Extra virgin olive oil, don't you watch Rachael Ray?"

"Who?" Murphy laughed as Tory's groan rumbled through the receiver. "Just kidding, I know who she is. Relax Tory, it's just dinner."

"It's much more than that and you know it. Have you showered?"

"In the ocean."

"Murphy," Tory growled with exasperation. "Clean the shrimp, clean yourself, set the table, and then call me back."

The phone clicked in his ear. "Bossy woman." Murphy dug out the colander and began to rinse the shrimp.

The chicken was sizzling on the grill, and a bottle of wine was breathing on the counter when he heard Jess's Jeep pull in. "Hey Jess, let yourself in," he called over the deck railing. "I'll meet you in the kitchen in a minute."

Jess slipped out of her sandals in the foyer and decided to satisfy her curiosity about the rental house on her way to the kitchen. The property was only a year old and had not lost the shiny-new feel. Pale ceramic tiles beckoned Jess toward the heart of the house where oiled pine planks emphasized the open floor plan. The large windows and high ceilings gave the home an even more spacious feel. In the family room, oversized bookcases and a fireplace added a homey charm. She looked through the glass deck doors where Murphy was busy at the grill and wandered toward the bar which separated the kitchen from the dining room.

The phone rang, startling her. She sat the salad she'd tossed together on the counter and on the third ring, she lifted the receiver. "Hello?"

"Well hello yourself. I'll assume you're Jess, since I know Murphy's expecting you."

"Yes, this is Jess. Should I take a stab and say this must be Tory?"

"Got it in one," Tory laughed, immediately liking Jess. "So if my baby brother's busy, tell me if he's cleaned the shrimp and set the table."

"Well I just got here…" Jess turned as Murphy strolled into the room.

"Don't let her rile you," Murphy smiled. "Tell her I'm clean, the shrimp are clean, and I didn't have time to call her back."

"Umm well..." Jess stammered. Tory's laughter filled her ear once again. Murphy held his hand out and Jess gratefully handed the receiver over.

"Hey Sis, Yeah I'm good, one question..." Murphy walked from the room. His voice dropped low and was muffled. Jess tried not to eavesdrop, but she was curious. A second later, he wandered back with a boyish gleam twinkling in his eyes. "Tory badgered me for your phone number and threatened to call you tomorrow for a full report. Tory said it's a girl thing," Murphy shrugged, "whatever that means. Is Riley settled in at Kate's?"

"Yep, board games and pie, he'll be good for hours."

"Perfect. You hungry?"

"That was a requirement, right? What can I help you with?"

Murphy held her gaze and moved purposely toward her. "You can do two things. First..." He pulled her hard against him and captured her mouth in a ravenous kiss. The heat shifted to tenderness just as quickly. Murphy eased her back, before he forgot he had more at stake than a simple dinner. He deliberately lightened his voice, "and second, pour us some wine while I check on the chicken."

They worked together in easy tandem to pull the meal together. Spinach fettuccini with sautéed shrimp and grilled chicken topped with fresh grated parmesan. "Murphy, this is sinful." Jess forked up another bite.

"I only make two things well."

"What's the other?"

"Lasagna."

"Yum."

"Save room for dessert."

"Oh, it's too late for that. I'm stuffed."

"We can wait a little bit." Murphy started to clear the dishes. "Stay sitting," Murphy told Jess as she starting to rise from her chair. "This will only take me a minute."

Feeling like a pampered woman, Jess poured herself another glass of wine. "Okay if I top off your glass?"

"Don't complain if I step on your toes when we get to the dancing portion of the evening."

"We aren't really going dancing, are we?"

"It was a requirement Jess," Murphy teased. "But we aren't going far." The dishwasher hummed to life and Murphy lifted his wine. "How about before we dance, we sit on the deck? We have about a half an hour until the mosquitoes won't allow it."

Jess smiled, "You're learning, Cowboy."

Murphy led Jess to the two-seated glider situated on the wide planks overlooking the bay. He balanced their wine glasses as Jess tucked her feet under her hip and snuggled in close. Murphy's long legs eased the glider back and forth, back and forth. They sat in silence watching the ripples chase across the bay surface as the early evening breeze raced the sun to the horizon.

The public boat dock, at the end of the road, was a hub of activity. Murphy and Jess watched as weary waterman tied off their boats and unloaded their gear. "Wonder if they had a good day?" Jess said.

"Any day fishin' is a good day, fish or no fish." Murphy grinned over at her, "I read that on a t-shirt at the airport." The soft rumble of an outboard engine hummed in the distance. "Here he comes," Murphy motioned toward the cove. Jess inched forward just as an eighteen foot, center console, vessel moved into view. "Every day, nearly to the minute, he comes to check his pots. I find it amazing."

Jess took pleasure in how observant Murphy was of the simple island life. "That's part of the reason I chose Chincoteague when I relocated. Small towns have their drawbacks, like one cinema and one book store, but they also have the quaintness and charm of a late day fisherman checking his traps." Jess sipped her wine. "Added to that, it's beautiful. Just look at that sky." The brilliant afternoon blue had faded gently to soft periwinkle, etched with peach and pink. Her voice softened, "I gambled moving here. I needed to know I could raise Riley my way, not park him in daycare while I slaved away in a city. I grabbed up the nature center job and now have a career with potential, and a proxy family. The jackpot was that Riley was young enough to adapt, and he loves it here. He has friends, Little League, and Boy Scouts..."

Murphy listened as Jess spelled out her hopes for Riley. Nowhere on her list did she mention anything for herself. He wondered if that was how it was for all mothers once the kids came along. All their energy and dreams, time, and money, channeled to the children. If any morsels were left over, then and only then, would a mother consider herself.

"Of course," Jess continued, "Riley has goals of his own. He has his heart set on owning a pony of his own, but last week he mentioned surfing." She laughed richly. "I should be able to hold him off on the pony, another year or two."

"Heck by then," Murphy said, "he'll be interested in girls."

"At ten!" Jess gasped.

"He's a late bloomer," Murphy patted her knee, "I was chasing skirts in pre-school."

"That doesn't surprise me," Jess chuckled.

Murphy finished his wine and stood. "Ready to head inside?" He extended his hand toward her.

Jess uncurled her legs and looked at Murphy, tall, strong, steady, silhouetted against the conclusion of nature's spectacular light show. She gently laid her hand in his, and allowed him to draw her up. She followed the momentum, lifted to her toes, and whispered a kiss across his cheek. "Thanks for a great evening."

"You're leaving?" Murphy didn't care for the panic that stirred inside him.

"No, I just wanted you to know now." She tipped her head up and smiled fully. "Mind if I give Kate a call? I need to check on Riley."

"Nope, take your time." Murphy slid the glass door open and stepped aside for Jess. The cool air conditioned air whooshed out. "Fire?"

"Why not."

"Meet you in the family room."

Murphy flipped the switch and the gas fireplace surged to life. Sure was easier than hauling logs, but not quite the same. Murphy enjoyed the muscle-straining work of cutting and splitting wood throughout the year. The pop of a dry piece of harvested timber could be its own kind of therapy after a cold day working outside.

Jess peeked at Murphy reclined on the overstuffed couch with head cradled in the plush cushions, his eyes closed. Soft music floated in the air, a country artist Jess recognized. The fire, the music, the meal...she didn't know how much more romance she could take. Looking at Murphy, bathed in firelight, waiting for her... She had hoped for fond memories, but what she was getting was a full heart and no future. She had allowed herself to spin fanciful dreams of happily-ever-after one other time in her life.

Her naive whims had been crushed by pretty words and empty promises. Dreams and expectations were for foolish young girls. Jess squared her shoulders, reminded herself she was no longer foolish, nor was she terribly young and stepped toward the couch.

"Everything okay over at Kate's?"

Keep it light, she coached herself, as she settled next to Murphy. "Riley is beating the pants off Rudy in Scrabble, which thrills my little game player. He doesn't take kindly to losing. Kate said Rudy and Riley have eaten two servings of dessert and will be snoring within the hour."

Murphy rolled his head toward her, "Does that mean you can stay longer?"

Jess swallowed the lump that had lodged in her throat and watched the flames dance in the fireplace. Dreams, she realized, didn't care how old you were and foolishness...well... "Yes, Murphy, I can stay," she sighed and rested her head on his shoulder.

They sat in silence as the curtain of darkness settled over the island. Murphy sipped his wine, "Jess can I ask you something?"

"Anything."

"You have all these adventures envisioned for Riley. What about you?"

She shrugged.

"How about before Riley? I know life can shift without warning and leave you scrambling to regain your balance. I also know that change can create an opportunity for something greater. For you, it brought Riley and island life; for me, the west and ranching. But before, when you had nothing but a blank canvas; what were your dreams for you?"

"Fairy tale stuff, Murphy. Little girl dreams: Being swept off my feet, live on a cloud with Prince Charming, a few kids, and a Chesapeake Bay Retriever." She laughed. "Then I had teenage visions of a power career and a gallant husband, elaborate dinner parties, tons of friends…"

Murphy shuddered, "Are those the standard hopes of young girls? It's no wonder we guys have it tough."

"You know what I mean," she punched him lightly. "Reality gave me a healthy dose, and I paid. In college I met someone who said the right things, promised me the foolishness, and turned out not to be free to fulfill any part of them." Jess sat quietly swirling the wine in her glass.

"I didn't tell Riley's father I was pregnant. I was alone when I went to the doctor's office to get my blood test results. There was an obviously pregnant woman in the waiting room beside me bubbling with anticipation over her upcoming marriage. I shared in her excitement wondering if I'd be planning a wedding myself within a matter of weeks. I realized during the conversation the man she was gushing about was the same man I had been involved with for the last year."

"Scum."

Jess hummed in agreement. "It took me a bit to get there, but yeah, scum." She reached forward and set her wine glass on the coffee table. "So pregnant, alone, and unbelievably frightened, I went home. I turned to my family who stunned me with their lack of support, and decided screw it. I am a self-sufficient woman, I can do this alone. I found a job in the mid-west working on an environmental education grant which grew to a career educating urban kids. You should see a child's face when he sees a tomato plant not only grow green from the earth but produce a bright shining piece of fruit that he can sink his teeth into."

Murphy smiled at the picture she painted. "You loved it."

"I did; but ultimately, I wanted Riley to be able to grow and play in different surroundings. I fell into the job here and well..." She lifted her shoulder, "You know the rest."

No, Murphy thought, he had barely scratched the surface of what he wanted to know about Jess and Riley. What he did know shook him to the soles of his ancient cowboy boots. This beautiful, courageous, compassionate woman was **the** woman. What he didn't know was how he was going to transition that knowledge into a future.

"You still haven't answered me, Jess. What do you, the self-sufficient happy-with-her-life woman want, just for you?"

"It's been a long time since I've even thought about that, Murphy." She considered a moment, "Career and security, of course," she paused, "a partner, someone who will love me, love Riley, and cherish us; someone who will want more children, and will savor each step with me; pregnancy, birth, and every second that follows. It's a process that is meant to be shared by two people..." Hearing it all out loud struck her funny. "Ha! Not asking for much, am I?"

"You want it all," Murphy leaned forward and set his wine glass aside. "Who doesn't?" The music changed and as the next song began, Murphy pushed up from the soft cushion. "Dance with me?"

"Here?"

"Here... barefooted in front of the fire, in an air conditioned house."

Jess allowed him to lead her around the coffee table. The soft flames from the fire glimmered into the corners of the dim room. Playfully, Murphy spun Jess under his arm, grinned at her. Jess allowed him to align her body with his. She rested her cheek on his shoulder and let the melody swirl around them. Murphy's strong arms banded securely around her and they swayed as one. The heat from the fire teased Jess's legs. The rhythmic pulse of the music bombarded her senses. A long breath drifted past her lips as Jess allowed herself to slip into the fantasy.

The day they'd spent together on the sand, the easy evening meal, unwinding on the deck, dancing barefooted in front of the fire... Jess felt tiny, fragile, cherished. She wasn't foolish enough to claim love, but that didn't stop the longing.

Murphy eased back and looked down into her face. Really looked. How in the world he had tripped over his future on a mistake of a vacation was beyond him. He lowered his forehead to hers.

Jess wrapped her arms tightly and held. "I do want everything, Murphy."

"So do I." He kissed her then, a brush of lips that declared without a word the depth of his emotions. In an incredibly romantic gesture, Murphy swept her into his arms and strode from the living room. Jess's hand rested over his hammering heart, her breath tickled his neck. He fumbled a bit given that the layout of the rental house was somewhat unfamiliar, but arrived unscathed in the bedroom.

Jess felt impossibly female. Carried away like the princess in her girlhood fantasy. The pale beams from the summer moon poured across the unlit room. Her breath hitched when Murphy's knees bumped the king sized bed. He looked intently at her, seemingly into her, a moment before he lowered his head, and with incredible sweetness, kissed her.

Absently, Murphy thought candles, music, Jess deserved those things. He gazed at her cradled in his arms, and his thoughts emptied.

The kiss spun out, better than any imagined castle in the sky. Jess was grateful she wasn't standing, certain she'd melt into a puddle of female mush without Murphy's support. Tenderly, without breaking the kiss, he laid her across the soft comforter and followed her down. Jess's hair fanned out across the soft spread. Her eyes glistened with the beauty of the moment. Murphy circled his thumbs across her cheeks and along her jaw, memorizing her features. Banking his need to plunder, he kissed her unhurriedly, wanting the moment to go on forever. His heart thundered in his chest. He too wanted it all, and he was certain that this was it. He strained to keep the words that screamed in his head from escaping his lips and offered what he knew in this moment she'd accept. Him.

Painstakingly slow, he removed her clothes and traced his work-roughened hands over her shoulders and along her ribs as if mesmerized by the sight of her skin.

"Murphy..." Jess sighed, as lost as he. She gripped his head and tugged him back to her. Eyes moist with the beauty of what they shared, she tumbled into the next soul shattering kiss.

CHAPTER TWENTY-FIVE

Jess wakened early. The sun, a tinge of pink, attempted to climb above the horizon. She slipped from the tangled sheets and as quietly as possible tiptoed into the luxurious master bath.

Murphy rolled over, stretched, and found her gone. His stomach tightened for a moment until he heard the shower running. If Jess thought she was going to escape without breakfast, she had another thing coming. He moved briskly, pulled on his lounge pants and set out for the kitchen. Thank heaven, and Joel, for the stocked fridge. Murphy flipped the oven on and slid a pan of crab quiche on the top rack. He set the oven timer, poured two glasses of orange juice, and hustled back to the bedroom.

Jess wrapped herself in a plush purple bath sheet. Decadence, she thought as the towel wrapped two complete circles around her body. If she could just grab her clothes and slip out, her perfect evening would be complete. Murphy would be leaving town in twenty-four hours and she needed to start to carve out some space so her heart would be able to survive when he was gone.

Jess stepped quietly into the bedroom, not wanting to disturb Murphy, only to find him standing framed in the window looking out over the breaking day. She was kidding herself. The time for regaining emotional distance was long gone. She moved toward him and slipped her arms around his waist. "Morning, I hope the shower didn't disturb you."

"Finding you gone from the bed disturbed me. I had plans for you and this sunrise we are about to witness.

"Mmm," she kissed his bare shoulder, "plans, huh?" Jess looked at the shades of yellow, peach, and pink hues bubbling at the horizon as the sun moved to take position in the sky.

"I wanted to hold you and watch an Eastern Shore sunrise." Murphy tugged Jess until she stood in front of him. Scrubbed and fresh from her shower, wrapped in a fluffy towel, her sodden hair across her collar bone. The words were in his throat. Words he had promised he wouldn't give any woman until he was certain the entire package would follow. Here she was; standing with a hint of a smile on her face before him.

Jess watched as Murphy fought some unspoken internal battle. "Hey Cowboy, no deep thoughts or we'll miss this incredible sunrise."

"I've decided to join it, rather than watch."

"Huh?"

"Make love with me, Jess...right now as the sun breaks into the day."

Jess loosened the towel and turned, slowly allowing the seemingly yards of fabric to unravel at her feet. Her smile brimmed with female confidence, "Oh yes, let's do that."

CHAPTER TWENTY-SIX

Jess loved the bay in the morning. She felt like an idiot for sneaking out of the rental house while Murphy was in the shower. She had eased her guilt by tossing a note on the counter that she had to pick up Riley. Cowardly behavior didn't sit well, but she needed to settle herself and allow the quiet of the bay to work its magic. The rising sun tickled the water's smooth surface as the aluminum boat puttered beneath the drawbridge. Jess guided the boat near the shoreline and into the cove that bordered Kate's property. She eased along the dock and tied off. Kate's house was still dark except for a faint light glow of the punched tin lantern hanging in the kitchen. Kate peeked out the screen door, "Coffee?" she mouthed soundlessly. Jess nodded and pointed to the glider on the deck.

Moments later Kate strolled across the deck holding two cups of coffee and a huge slice of peach pie. Jess accepted the mug, then laughed as Kate pulled two forks from her pocket. The women sat in silence as the glider rocked gently. The pie disappeared and Kate set the plate aside. "Well sweetie, how's your heart?" Jess leaned until her head rested on Kate's shoulder. "Turn your brain off for ten minutes," Kate patted Jess's knee. "Finish your coffee, breathe in and out. Take one thing at a time, Jessie girl, one thing at a time."

Jess stared at the bottom of her empty cup. "I thought I could handle a fling, Kate." Jess shook her head. "I'm in love with him," she said miserably and buried her face in her hands.

"Who could blame you?"

"He lives in Montana! Not Maryland, Delaware or even anywhere on the entire East Coast! Montana. I can't possibly uproot my life and start from scratch with no stability. It's not fair to Riley or even the Nature Center. I can't possibly even consider it."

"Seems like you've done just that before, uproot, start from scratch. Seems to me it's turned out pretty well for you."

"You know what I mean, Kate," Jess sighed.

"I'll tell you what I do know. I watched a twenty-something girl roll across the Bay Bridge with a Jeep loaded full of guts and an angelic, high strung five-year old. I watched that girl ask for nothing but an honest shake as she worked damn hard to build her boy a foundation he could stand on. Riley's more than lucky to have you, he's blessed. What you've built under him has nothing to do with the state he lives in, and everything to do with his Momma being happy."

"Taking on a mother and a child is not what Murphy was planning on."

"Planning for a future doesn't have a lot to do with what life deals you. You roll, adjust, and make new, or you stand still and stay living solid secure while you wait for whatever geography gives you." Kate took Jess's face into her caring hands. "Every woman makes choices that change her path. If you ask me, you are selling yourself and Riley short. You deserve it all Jess. If Murphy is the one, the details will fall in."

"I just don't want to make a decision based on thirteen days of sun and fun with a passing-through Saltwater Cowboy. I'd feel like a fool if I bet on a mirage, you know? What if I've conjured these feelings out of loneliness?"

"Only you know deep inside," Kate squeezed Jess's knee. "Want some more coffee? Riley will be stirring in a little bit."

Jess tipped her face to the sun, "Coffee would be great, one thing at a time right?"

"That's my girl."

CHAPTER TWENTY-SEVEN

Murphy leaned over the corral's highest rail. The paint foal eyed him as he lengthened his neck toward Murphy's outstretched hand.

"Makin' friends?" Rudy moseyed over and joined Murphy.

"Giving it a shot."

"Bold one, ain't he?"

"Bold doesn't bother me. I like 'em confident and spunky." The paint snorted and tossed his head.

"He's got your number all right," Rudy laughed as the foal edged closer.

Murphy turned his hand over, revealing the sugar cube he had palmed. "Stealin' your tricks," he winked at Rudy, and then turned his attention back to the foal. "Come on in little buddy...that's it." Murphy coaxed.

"Two more steps and you got him." Rudy watched the exchange.

"Not going to be today," Murphy whispered. "Momma's got a bead on me."

On cue, the painted mare whinnied loudly, scolding her tot. The foal trotted to his mother's side and began to nurse. "She's not as protective as I'd expect." Murphy observed the mare as she stood beside the stable door.

"She's not her best today. Pulled up lame this morning," Rudy said. "We're watching her."

"That happen often?"

"Some ponies get bumped a bit during sorting, but no, it doesn't happen often. Sometimes they become agitated as the foals are sold. Add to that the carnival noise and all the people," Rudy shrugged. "We'll observe her. Vet will too. At least she'll have a few months to relax 'til Jr's picked up." Rudy pulled out his tobacco pouch. "If she can't be returned to the herd, well then..."

"Well then, what?" Murphy regarded Rudy carefully.

"Beach living is hard enough without a leg weakness," Rudy raised his shoulder. "You live on a ranch Murphy; you know the choices that sometimes have to be made. But she's got some time."

Murphy looked over at the mare and nursing foal. It was the part of owning livestock he hated most. When the animals got hurt or sick...it never sat well with him. "Don't make any decisions without including me in the conversation. All right?"

Rudy tipped his head and acknowledged Murphy. Damned if he didn't like the man.

Riley raced over, startling the ponies. "Easy Sporto," Rudy said and lifted him to stand on the fence slats.

"Sorry, just wanted to see Montana."

"She's beside the stable, lying down."

"I'm going to go let her smell my stink."

Rudy and Murphy chuckled as Riley started to run, then corrected himself and moved in an enormous, slow, exaggerated steps.

"Hey men," Jess called as she walked toward them. She had decided, following her conversation with Kate, to seek Murphy out and stop being a coward. He only had one more day on the island and even if their affair ended when his plane took off, she wasn't going to play a part in having it end badly. "Why the long faces?" Jess propped her elbows on the rail and studied Rudy and Murphy.

"The mare pulled up lame this morning." Rudy inclined his head toward the pony. "Cowboy here's going soft on me. He might need a hanky."

Jess poked Rudy in the ribs, "Knock it off. There's nothing wrong with soft."

"I'm not soft," Murphy scoffed.

"Oh look, there's my favorite. He's so beautiful," Jess admired the paint foal. "Private bidder sign for him yet?"

Rudy raised a questioning brow at Murphy, who shrugged. "Yes..." Rudy answered hesitantly, "He's signed for."

"Darn. I was hoping he'd be stranded. If I was going to go soft on any foal this year, it would have to be that one."

"Riley wearing you down?" Murphy smiled, "Damn that kid's good."

Jess pinned him with a stern look. "I am just saying if the paint was stranded, I'd have considered talking to Sean about some corral space."

Murphy snickered, "Thanks for clearing that up."

Rudy cackled, "Not wearing you down, ha!"

"Men." Jess seethed and stalked away.

"She's something else, isn't she?" Murphy watched Jess march off.

"Yeah, she sure is. I take it she doesn't know that foal is going cross country with you."

"No, and I'd prefer to keep it that way."

"Your business," Rudy shook his head, "Your business. You're coming to the firehouse tonight, right? A fierce cookout to close the festival."

"Heard something about it," Murphy smiled.

"Tradition requires we eat well to finalize this year's penning." Rudy wiggled his brows, "Not seafood this time but traditional pit barbeque. Beef, chicken, ribs...de-lish."

"Sounds great." Murphy's eyes tracked to where Jess sat in the straw beside Riley talking to Montana. Not exactly how he'd hoped to spend his last night on the island. But if he had to be surrounded by firefighters, good food, and music, he hoped Jess at least would be there.

"You gonna' stand and stare at her, or walk over and invite the girl?" Rudy startled Murphy.

"I figured she'd probably be there, right?"

"Pansy," Ruddy shook his head. "You want to take her west with you boy-o, you better keep up the offense. Give a woman too much time to think, she'll build all kinds of walls mortared together with rational thinking." Rudy's full body shuddered.

"Just trying to let her work through it at her own pace."

"Understandable," Rudy said, but what he wanted to say was, stupid. "I gotta' get on. I'll see you tonight."

Murphy moved around the corral. Riley grinned up at him, "She let me stroke her nose. Can you believe that?"

"Good job, you keep visiting her regular, she'll start to look forward to seeing you." Murphy said.

Jess gripped the railing and pulled herself up, "Hey Riley, that trough could use some fresh water. Turn the hose on slowly and top it off for Montana and her friends."

"Cool." Riley rushed around the back of the stable.

Jess brushed the straw from her pants. "Sorry I took off this morning."

His heart had sunk when he discovered her gone. "It's okay, I saw your note." He graciously let her off the hook. Murphy reached out and toyed with her fingers. "Jess, last night was... I just have never... Are we okay?"

Jess looked into Murphy's eyes and found them swimming with emotion. Her heart relaxed; he felt the same. She wrapped her arms around him and clung; incredibly relieved to not be suffering alone. "I feel like an idiot Murphy. I decided you were safe to have dinner and a fling with."

"I'm flattered," his laugh tickled against her cheek, "I guess."

"But I'm not a fling girl, Murphy. I can't uproot Riley. I just...It's too complicated." The circumstances hadn't changed and Jess felt the heaviness crawl back into her chest, "I should just go, it's getting harder," Lost for words, she waved her hands between them and stepped back. "I can't, I need to go."

"No Jess," Murphy grabbed her hands as she started to back away. "We can figure something out."

She shot him a sassy smile but didn't quite pull it off. "We have our integrity Murphy. If we try to bend reality and make it work, we'll just wind up frustrated and twist something beautiful into something sour." She lifted her hands despairingly. "I need to remember beautiful...I need to go. Please don't make it harder." Jess kissed his cheek and hurried away.

Murphy watched as she gathered Riley, even as he protested that he wasn't done watering the ponies, and led him off the grounds. He gripped the corral like a lifeline and lowered his head until it rested on his forearm. "What am I going to do," he muttered to himself. "What do I do now?"

CHAPTER TWENTY-EIGHT

The firehouse buzzed with activity. There appeared to be as many people celebrating the end of penning as there had been the start. The backyard was lined once again with tables and chairs. Rotisseries, burdened with meat, spun above leaping flames in an open fire pit. Tantalizing scents filled the air, whetting the crowd's appetite for the feast.

·Murphy sat at a long table surrounded by Sean, Bobby, Nub, Boots and Rudy. The men lifted a toast to the success of the penning, then another to friendship. Laughter rolled, jokes flew... Rudy had been dead on, Murphy thought; the barbeque was the ideal way to wrap the events of the last days.

"Cowboy," Rudy smiled a devilish smile. "Since you didn't do too bad for a westerner, we got something for you."

"Gee thanks," Murphy said sarcastically.

"I speak for the gang when I say, we'd like to see you come 'round our way again." The men muttered their agreement. "Penning or not, you're welcome, anytime," Rudy tossed a canvas fireman's bag across the table. The sack was stamped with bold black letters across the front, ROOKIE. "Just dump it out," Rudy instructed.

The contents of the bag plopped across the table. Murphy lifted a pink Penning Event Staff T-shirt from the pile, signed by all the firefighters. Next, he saw a deck of cards with a ten dollar bill taped to the top and an invitation to play poker at Sean's.

"You owe me more than ten, buddy," Murphy laughed. The rest of the pile consisted of a plush toy horse with the markings like Buzz, a plastic container holding a piece of peach pie, a baggie of sand and shells, and in the spirit of masculine humor a live blue crab scooted across the table and dropped into the grass.

The men hollered with laughter as Murphy jumped to the side. Nub snared the fleeing crab as it attempted escape. "Wanna take him home with ya?" Nub wagged the furious crab at Murphy, "or would you like to donate him to the fine fare we'll be eating in an hour?"

"Only you would bother to cook one measly crab," Bobby snorted.

Nub turned the crab toward his face, "He called you measly. You gonna' take that?"

Bobby was already pushing from the table as Nub rounded the corner holding the blue crab out in front claws snapping. Bobby sprinted across the lawn with Nub hot on his heels.

"Boys," Rudy lifted his beer, "Play nice."

"I'm going to miss you guys. This was a great experience," Murphy said sincerely.

"Hallmark's on the line," Sean taunted.

Murphy cleared his throat, "Anyone want to try to take the westerner down at horseshoes before the meal's ready?" Challenge thrown down, the table emptied and the men took turns at the sand pits with Murphy.

It was sundown before Jess pulled her Jeep onto the firehouse parking lot. She'd purposely delayed her arrival, hoping Riley would fall asleep and give her an opportunity to skip the festivities altogether. She had done laundry, given Poncho a much needed bath, and scrubbed the kitchen until it gleamed. The surge of energy had done nothing but tire Jess and irritate Riley.

"Okay little man," Jess set the brake and turned off the engine. "I am not sure how long we are staying, so no fussing when I tell you time's up."

"Yes Momma," Riley gripped the door handle, "Can I go?"

Jess nodded and he took off like a shot disappearing around the building. "You are not gutless Jess," she told herself. "He'll be gone in the morning. Suck it up."

"Talking to yourself?"

Jess jumped, then relaxed when she saw Kate strolling her way. "I'll talk to you when my heart settles. Whew, you startled me."

"I was afraid you weren't going to show."

"It crossed my mind," Jess smiled weakly, "But Riley wouldn't let up."

"It's been an unforgettable year for him." Kate opened Jess's door. "Now take a deep breath and get your tuckous out of that Jeep and join the party."

Jess allowed Kate to lead her into the backyard, then feed her until she thought she'd burst. Jess had scanned the crowd and found Murphy involved in a tight contest of horseshoes. If things went her way, he'd stay occupied and she'd be able to .slink out without having to face him again.

A clanging bell disrupted the noise of the party. Rudy stood on the back steps of the firehouse. "Sorry to interrupt the festivities folks, but we got to take care of the business of the night. Thank you never seems to cover it, and I am not about to call you all off by name. What I will say is the penning was a success once again. The fund raising goals were met, new friends were made, and memories were captured that will last a lifetime. Now if you can all stay quiet long enough, we'll enjoy a photo presentation our computer whizzes have put together. I think the pictures will sum up this speech better than I ever could. Thank you." Rudy moved from the steps and the outside lights were turned off, leaving just the lawn torches burning along the property's edge.

Jess crossed the yard and gathered Riley, "Come stand with me by the fence. I think you'll enjoy the photo show."

The firefighters had hung a bed sheet from the second floor windows, creating a large viewing screen. The first picture projected was a fabulous image of Rudy standing in front of the young rookies. The image captured twelve boys seated on hay bales listening intently to Rudy's instructions for the penning event. A few moments later, the picture faded and was replaced with one of Sean leaning confidently on the top rail of the corral. People offered commentary as the photos switched again and again. The collage represented all facets of the event. Kate serving pie, ponies being herded, joyful spectators, the parade...

Jess's breath hitched as Murphy and Riley's faces filled the sheet. The picture, the one she had taken after the pony swim, captured the pair as they leaned forward with apples jammed between their teeth and the horses on either side nipping the red fruit. Ooos, ahhs, and laughter circulated through the folks on the lawn. Jess blinked the sentiment from her eyes as Riley bounced up and down seeing himself on the big screen.

In the middle of the yard, Murphy accepted the firemen's playful heckles, but couldn't seem to take his eyes from the picture. Feelings, unexplainable feelings, rushed through him from head to toe. This is it, he thought. That moment in life that scares you brainless. As the picture transitioned, Murphy stood and his eyes swept the lawn. The noise of the party faded and he zeroed in on Jess. Seeing only her, he strode purposefully to where she stood at the back of the yard with Kate and Riley.

Jess, thunderstruck by the intensity on Murphy's face, gripped Riley's shoulders.

"Oh my," Kate fanned herself, captivated as Murphy's determined stride carried him across the lawn. "My, my, my..."she said breathlessly.

"Murphy!" Riley vibrated with excitement. "Did you see us? Did you?"

Murphy blinked as Riley snapped him from his trance. He turned his attention to Riley, kneeled in the grass, and said, "I saw it all right, and I hope to get a copy to take home."

"Momma took it."

"I know. Would you mind if I borrowed your Mom for a little bit?"

Riley stuck his hand on his hip and scrutinized Murphy. "You going to make out?"

"Riley," Jess hissed.

Murphy looked directly into the young eyes and answered seriously, "If I'm lucky, I was hoping to do just that."

"I'll never understand it." Riley shook his head. Kate fought the urge to laugh while Jess stood with her mouth gaping. Murphy nodded solemnly at Riley, as if understanding his opinion. Riley studied Murphy and then looked at his mother's face. With a simple shrug he said, "Suit yourselves, but I'm not going to watch. Kate, you want to grab a soda and a seat, and leave these two to their business?"

Kate roared, "Can't tell he's been hanging with the men, can you?"

Jess rolled her eyes skyward, "I'm sorry Kate, I've been imposing on you so much lately."

"Nonsense," Kate pulled Riley tight to her side, "Go grab me a diet pop and a chair my boy." She turned to Jess and gathered her close. "Riley is no imposition." She hugged tightly and whispered, "No argument 'cause I'm about to meddle. I am keeping your little man overnight. No, no" Kate said before Jess's protest even passed her lips. "Tend your business and listen to the man. He may just surprise you." Kate eased back and brushed her hand over Jess's cheek, and with a quick wink to Murphy, sauntered off after Riley.

Murphy and Jess eyed each other nervously. Everything he'd wanted to say dried up on his tongue. She stood close enough to touch, yet felt unreachable.

"If you really want a copy of that photo, I'll send it out." Jess dipped her head.

"Of course I want it." Murphy shifted his feet, "I thought you weren't going to come tonight."

"Almost didn't." Jess smiled sheepishly, "Riley bugged me for an hour, and I ran out of excuses. Cowardly behavior doesn't suit me Murphy."

"I think there are a lot of things you could be, but I don't think being a coward could ever be one of them." Her eyes locked on his. "Could we go inside Jess? I'd like to speak to you without an audience."

Jess peered over his shoulder and noted that in fact, several pairs of eyes and ears were focused in their direction. "Give me a minute."

Murphy watched Jess cross the lawn to Kate and Riley. She leaned down talking quietly, first to Riley, then to Kate. She kissed each of their cheeks and turned her green eyed gaze to Murphy.

Power punched through him as he watched her move purposefully through the crowd, each confident stride bewitching him further.

She reached out her hand, threaded her fingers through his, and tugged. "Come with me, Cowboy," she said and led him around the side of the firehouse. The shadows of the building enveloped them. She calculated and took three more steps to assure their privacy before she whirled and leapt much like the night they'd met, fusing her mouth hungrily to his.

Murphy's fingers gripped her hips as the momentum spun them until they slammed against the firehouse. A groan of raw pleasure escaped from deep within him.

Jess moaned in answer as the warmth of the bricks seeped into her spine. She slid her hands up to cup Murphy's face, her fingers feathered over his features, tracing his jaw, his cheeks. "You did say you wanted to make out, right?" she said breathlessly. "How was that for starters?"

"Fine…just fine," Murphy nipped her bottom lip.

"I'd like to take you somewhere Murphy. Will you come with me?"

"Mmmhmm," Murphy kissed her until she giggled.

"You'll have to put me down."

"In an hour or so," Murphy was persistent. Jess playfully smacked his shoulder. "You…started…this," he said accenting each word with another quick kiss.

"Yeah well, I hope to finish it too… but not with an audience of one hundred and my son around the corner."

"Fair enough." Murphy stole one final kiss and settled her feet back on the ground. "Lead on."

CHAPTER TWENTY-NINE

Jess drove through the side-streets and alleys of the peaceful town. She navigated the dark roads like the local she'd become. The Jeep slowed, and Jess pulled onto a sandy lane. Illuminated in the headlights was a small house with bright pink shutters and a long screened porch. The house was dark, the lawn unkempt, and in a shadow at the rear of the property was a scarred wooden dock. Jess shut off the engine and set the brake.

"The first day Riley and I arrived on the island I canvassed every street to get a feel for small community living." Murphy looked at her profile as she studied the home. "I got lost more times than I care to admit," she continued, "and I turned around at least five times in this very driveway. At the time, a couple in their thirties owned the house and they had an adorable little boy. The flower beds were charming, toys littered the lawn, and a pontoon boat was tied at the dock." Jess took a moment and pulled the picture from her memory. "A family lived here, was happy here. I wanted that for Riley. I wanted a secure place where a family builds memories." Jess took a deep breath. "I dug in Murphy. Determination and a modest savings account were all I had to build on. Two years ago, the couple relocated to Maryland for business, and decided to rent the house as a vacation property. Kate heard, through the island network of gab, they are selling it after this season. This is the house I dreamed of owning. I want to build what they had for me and Riley."

Murphy knew she was telling him, showing him, all of this to let him down easy. He was going to be her fling after all. His heart sank. Hoping he didn't choke on the lump that had lodged in his throat, he said, "I admire you for knowing what it is you want and setting out to achieve it. My mom had to make the kinds of choices you are talking about. She moved across the country to give Tory and me a shot at a new life. You think I don't get what you're telling me? I do. I absolutely do." His heart was bleeding in his chest. "You and Riley deserve everything. Every damn thing."

"I can't see it," Jess said quietly. "I'm looking so hard and I just don't see it."

Murphy turned in his seat, "You've lost me, Jess."

"I've driven to this property countless times. Sat in this driveway just like this and envisioned my future. Riley playing in the yard; planting tomatoes, caring for flower beds...something has changed." Jess faced Murphy. "It's crazy. It's impulsive, and so unlike me, Murphy."

"Buying a property you set your eyes on three years ago is hardly impulsive."

She reached over and lifted Murphy's hand in hers. Gently she stroked her fingers over his palm. "I see it all; Riley playing, picnics, vegetable gardens... my life. I see it all so clearly Murphy, but only when I am looking at you." Jess held her breath. It was as if she stepped off a cliff and was falling and falling.

Murphy's eyes fluttered closed. He replayed Jess's words in his head. He waited for her to qualify her statement; positive a *however* or a *never-the-less* would come out of her mouth at any second. He wasn't afraid of much, but at the moment, he was terrified he had heard her wrong.

"Murphy?" Jess brushed her hand over his cheek, "Don't say anything. I'm sorry I dumped all that on you and I shouldn't have..."

Murphy's eyes flew open and the pool of emotion brimming there overwhelmed her. "Shh," Murphy pressed her hand firmly to his face, then pulled it to his lips. "I thought you were showing me this house to let me down easy. You were killing me in pieces, Jess."

He linked his fingers through hers. Choices he thought, choices could make or break a relationship. "I have always been a worst case scenario man. If I can live with the worst possible outcome of my choice, then it's worth the risk. If I can't swallow the worst, then the risk is too great." Murphy looked intently into Jess's eyes. Worry vanished and hope bloomed. Jess's grip tightened and he continued, "The life I knew to satisfy me, the life I envisioned myself being happy with for years now seems incomplete. I never expected you to uproot Riley and give up your career and the life you've made on a cowboy you've known for thirteen days. I was prepared to go back home and wait every day for you to come and visit, or come and stay, for the rest of your life. I'm in love with you, Jess. I'm in love with your son; I want him to be mine. I want to make our own breed of rascals…"

Jess silenced any further declaration with her lips clamped to his.

Seated in a Jeep, on the lawn of an island cottage, their dreams of family, and visions of future, were born.

EPILOGUE

The October breeze kicked across the island. The deserted fairground resembled a mid-west ghost town. Murphy eased the paint foal into the trailer behind his mother. Her leg weakness had been enough to grant her a pampered life in Montana with her tot. "Gonna' be a long ride, little one," Murphy said gently. "But when you and your momma see the ranch, I promise you, it will have been worth it."

"How we doing in there?" Jess asked.

Murphy stepped from the trailer, wrapped his arms around his new bride, and indulged himself in a lingering kiss. "Be ready to go shortly, Riley?" he called.

"Yeah Dad," Riley grinned proudly. It sounded so good to hear that word roll out of his mouth.

"Go round up Kate and Rudy, we're pulling out." Riley disappeared into the stable.

Murphy's cell phone rang. "Tory, I'd bet," Jess smiled.

Murphy checked the display, "You take it, I have one quick thing I need to take care of."

"Hi Tory...Yes in a few minutes, the ponies are loaded, and Riley's saying his goodbyes. Alright...yep, we'll call when we pull off for the night. Love you too." Jess clicked off and absorbed the amazement that her life had become in three short months.

"Girly," Rudy called out, "I got snacks for your ride." Rudy held Poncho on a tight leash in one hand and a canvas tote filled with snack crackers, nuts and juice boxes in the other. "Long trip you've got ahead. I hope you wander back our way from time to time."

Jess banded her arms tightly around the man who had come to mean so much to her. "You know you can come see us too."

"I know." Rudy squeezed, "Be happy, Sweetheart."

Jess had tears before she could stop them. "I am happy. He makes me so happy."

"Enough of that, you two," Kate walked over holding Riley's hand in hers. Jess could see that Kate's eyes too were shimmering.

"Momma, look at the books Kate got for me." Riley lifted a backpack filled with word finds, sudoku, drawing tablets, and crayons.

"That's wonderful. Put them in the truck, honey." Jess moved to Kate and wrapped her arms around her. "What am I going to do when I need a hug?"

"You are going to pick up the phone and we'll talk our way through it," Kate sighed. "And if that doesn't work, I'll get on a plane."

"Good." Jess pulled back as a truck pulled up beside the stable. "Is Sean picking up Montana today too?" Jess asked.

"If he is, he forgot his trailer," Rudy said. "Hey boy-o, what 'cha up to?"

"Came to see Murphy and Jess off," Sean strode across the lawn. "Where's Riley?"

"Right here!" Riley jumped from the truck. "Sean will you send me pictures of Montana as she gets bigger?"

"I don't think so," Sean said.

Riley's pout was instantaneous, "Well why not?"

"Because…" Sean looked over his shoulder. Murphy stood behind the group with Montana in a halter. "Don't go crazy or you'll spook her. Montana's going with you."

Riley's jaw dropped open. "She's going with me?" His voice was barely audible.

"Yep," Sean grinned broadly. "Your Dad and I worked it out. Can I come and visit her sometime?"

Riley nodded slowly as he stared.

"Help me out here, buddy?" Murphy held the rope out to Riley. "Easy now, walk her to the trailer, don't hesitate, just step right in. Put her in the stall behind the paint."

Murphy followed Riley to the trailer. Jess's vision blurred as she looked over at Kate and Rudy who blinked and sniffled respectively.

The truck eased off the fairgrounds and with a toot of the horn, Murphy, Jess, Riley, and Poncho set out for Montana. Kate lowered her waving hand as the truck disappeared from view, "Young love." She sighed.

"Young fools," Rudy snickered, "They have no idea what's ahead, and they couldn't care less."

"It's romantic." Kate poked him. "We meddle well, don't we?"

"I think you and I could do more than meddle."

"Do you now?" Kate quipped. "You sure took your damn sweet time."

Rudy huffed.

"Now don't get your back up," Kate patted his arm, "We're too old to circle much longer. Want to take a chance on an old gal?"

"I think I'm gambler enough." Rudy stepped close and kissed her lightly. Kate blushed like a school girl. "Pretty Kate, are you really going to give me a chance to win your heart?"

"Silly man," she laid her hand on his cheek. "If you had been paying attention, you'd have realized you had it all along."